THE ONE WHO GOT AWAY

For Mom and Dad,
Thanks for being my greatest cheerleaders.

~~~

Special thanks to Laura Davis.

Chapter 1

Gwen Trueblood slid the glass door open and stepped into the cool night air, sniffing greedily at the pungent scent of damp earth that greeted her. She felt the dew on the deck boards beneath her bare feet and smiled, her thin top lip sliding over its too-full counterpart.

Mornings were her favorite time of day, the hours before sunrise a seemingly magical gift reserved for those who appreciated their wonder. It was in this time that she did her best work, her mind free from the hazards of daily living and at once completely her own.

Already her fingers longed to drag a brush, heavy with paint, along the textured surface of a canvas. She would work on the last of an acrylic series she was doing for a show in New York. It was an abstract grouping, and she had yet to decide what she wanted to do for the last installment, having spent the better part of yesterday layering it with a background of the deepest purples and blues.

Images flipped through her mind as she sipped her hot coffee. A tree, its green leaves silhouetted against a darkened sky. A pond, at the edge of a forest. A storm.

A storm.

Dancing wind and the smell of coming electricity, the sky just beginning to mist. An image of her niece's new husband came to mind. Hank Jared's spirit was strong and good, a force to be reckoned with. She would include his energy in the painting, fighting the storm that surrounded him.

Decided now, she headed inside the old farmhouse, turning on lights as she went.

Sitting in front of her largest easel, she reached for her palette and paints. Her steady hand layered black and white onto the purple surface, instantly transforming it from a simple solid color to a turbulent scene. With broad strokes she worked a mass of red acrylic into the canvas with a thick butter knife. She spread it in large swirls, its texture like buttercream frosting piled high atop a cake.

The picture before her was now a swirling purple background with a red structure near the top. Turning her head to the side, Gwen considered with her eyes before reaching to blend a blue and a sea green into a vibrant, singing turquoise. She began to apply the paint to the canvas in a similar shape, this time in the bottom right corner. The energy of the color against the stormy background reminded her of David, and she smiled contentedly as she worked to make the shape more soothing in appearance, with rounded edges and a thick substance of acrylic.

When Gwen looked at the canvas, she didn't see the blocks of color that made up the composition. She saw Hank Jared and David Beaumont, riding out a storm. The energy of the piece felt right, but something was missing. Perusing the metal tubes of paint, her eyes landed on a peacock green and she froze, the image of Colin Mitchell invading her memory.

He'd been wearing a polo shirt exactly that color the day everything changed. She picked the tube up and held it, the warmth of her hands quickly heating the metal. It wasn't the first time she'd thought of him, though she usually pushed the memories aside as quickly as they surfaced. Instead, she twisted off the cap and squeezed a small amount onto her fingers, spreading it between her thumb and forefinger.

It was a beautiful color, at once intense and lovely, and she stared at it, remembering Colin's handsome face. The younger brother of David's best friend Rowan, Colin was a college student when he lived at their grandmother's house just north of New York City. Rowan had parties there the summer Gwen and David were dating, the short train ride along the Hudson River seeming to take them away to a magical land.

Another memory threatened, and Gwen wiped the color onto her apron before it could breathe new life into its lungs, but she was not willing to forsake the color. Using a tapered brush she worked it into the hairs and began to paint. With every stroke, the door she had firmly closed on Colin memory eased apart another crack, exposing something raw and base beneath.

Her cheeks heated as she remembered the warm golden brown of his eyes, staring into hers, the light summer's breeze picking up his dark hair and ruffling his shirt. But it was the way he looked at her, and the sheer attraction she felt pulling her to him that she remembered now.

They were standing on the patio overlooking the Hudson River on the evening of a glorious summers day. Where the others had gone, she did not know.

Are you with David? he asked.

She could hear the baritone of his voice, not a child at all, but a grown man. There was an understanding between them already that if she was alone, she would be his, and she thrilled at the flirtation. A wind gusted, holding her caftan firmly against her body, and she reached up to tuck her hair behind her ear. This man was appealing, but she was very much in love with someone else.

I am, she answered, a smile on her face and pride in her voice. His intense eyes never left hers as he raised his glass and nodded once, making her belly tingle.

There had been other parties after that one, and Colin was always there in the background, keeping his distance from Gwen. On her way to the final party of the summer with David, Gwen stared out the train window at the miles of passing river, its expanse glimmering in the late afternoon sun, and her pulse raced a little faster, knowing they would soon see Colin.

The admission was difficult for Gwen, though she recognized lust for what it was, and not some deeper betrayal of the man she loved. As the train rocked down the track, bringing her closer to him, she allowed herself to do what she had never done before. She fantasized about Colin Mitchell.

Gwen molded the paint into a textured construction as she allowed herself to remember her dreams of touching that young sexy boy with her hands like she now touched his energy with her brush.

She was flushed, goose bumps rising up on her arms and legs as she worked. This was dangerous territory, an area of her memory that should be cordoned off with hazard tape and left well enough alone. But Gwen delved deeper, her eyes briefly closing as she imagined Colin's lips at the side of her neck, much as she had on that train ride fifteen years before.

She heard herself breathing deeply, felt her lips fall apart. It had been a dream, a daydream, a mistake. The past and the present mingled and danced, finally free from the confines of her mind and forever emblazoned on the canvas. Gwen rested her brush on her palette and stared at her creation.

By the time she and David got to the party, Gwen had nearly forgotten about the dream. She got herself a glass of wine while David went off with Rowan to play cards, then stepped onto the veranda to enjoy the stunning views and the cool summer breeze.

She could feel Colin's presence the moment he joined her on the patio, though she did not turn around. Her body remembered her dreams of this man, every nerve in her body tingling in anticipation like a schoolgirl with an overwhelming crush. She was being silly, playing with fire, never considering she might be burned.

His voice was deep and vibrated in her belly. "I had a dream about you."

She heard his footfalls approach, could hear him breathing behind her. "You did?"

It was little more than a whisper when he spoke. "A daydream."

Shame swept up the back of her neck. She'd been caught, like a child. She had poked the lion with a stick and now he stood so close to her, poised to attack.

"It was so real..." he said.

Gwen raised her hand. "Don't." She hadn't meant to betray David, would never have done it if she'd known Colin was aware.

His voice was throaty and snaked up her arms. "And so damn good."

She was horrified at what she had done, but at the same time she wanted Colin to touch her. She could feel the need coming off him in waves, the answering echo in her own body begging him to do it.

"Colin!" Rowan's voice behind them was sharp, startling her.

Colin's voice dripped with annoyance. "Yes?"

"I need your help inside."

They all knew he was lying. She was so embarrassed. When she was able, she turned and faced Rowan, avoiding Colin's stare. "Is it something I can help with?" she asked, crossing the patio and heading into the house.

What have I done?

Gwen cursed herself and her damn libido, her attraction to this boy and her stupid response when he called her on it. She should have slapped him across the face. Isn't that what an innocent woman would do?

That's probably why it never occurred to you.

She found David in the basement, telling him she wasn't feeling well and wanted to go home, neither of which was a lie. That night, she lay in bed beside David and stared at the ceiling, explaining to the universe in general and to Colin Mitchell in particular that what had happened between them would never, ever, happen again.

Her eyes dropped from the easel to her bright green fingertips. Until she painted a peacock green glob on a stormy purple canvas, it had not.

~~~

Hank Jared pulled into the driveway of the old white farmhouse, the dread that had been brewing for days settling in his stomach like an anchor. In his mind's eye, David sat beside him in the passenger seat, leaning forward in eager anticipation. Which was weird, considering Gwen's husband David was dead, and Hank had never even met the man.

Hank forced his eyes open wide and blinked several times. He was losing it. It was a long drive from South Carolina to Vermont, and his legs ached to stand. He picked up a manila envelope, tracing his fingers down its creased edge. The papers inside had occupied his conscience for too long, their delivery now far overdue. They brought news of events unimaginable, and he deeply regretted that he would be the one to share their secrets with his friend.

He bided his time, surveying the landscape. Two more homes were visible in the distance, the rolling hills that separated them lined with long rail fences and old oak trees. Gwen's house stood tall and narrow, with a wide front porch and gingerbread trim. A green porch swing swayed invitingly in the warm summer breeze, and Hank imagined Gwen and David cuddled upon it, gently rocking as couples do.

Opening the door, Hank was hit with the scent of a recent rain shower and the heavy sweetness of summer flowers. It seemed only right that Gwen's house should smell like Mother Nature's very own. He often thought of his wife's aunt as a flower child stuck in the wrong generation.

The windows of the farmhouse were open, their curtains blowing in the warm morning breeze. He sighed heavily. At least she was home, and this would be the end of it. A fat yellow dog stood from where it had been laying on the wet grass, its tail wagging happily at Hank.

"Hey, Zeke." He bent to pet the animal. "Where's your mama?"

Chapter 2

"What if they find me?" asked the man, his shoulders hunched and his eyes wide. The tracks of recent tears were visible on his cheeks.

Colin felt sorry for him. It was one thing to sit across the table from a mobster or a drug runner. Javier Martinez was an academic who had been in the wrong place at the wrong time. Colin leaned back in his chair and gave his most confident look. "They won't. But if you are ever threatened, you call us and we move you immediately."

"My family..."

"Your wife and kids can come, too."

Martinez looked into his lap.

Picking up his coffee, Colin took a sip and waited. It was a difficult decision to wrap your head around. He had often wondered if he himself could do it—walk away from everyone he knew, leave behind all that he had worked for and start completely over.

Martinez raised his head and fixed Colin with a penetrating stare. "Has anyone in the program ever been killed?"

"No one who followed the rules has ever been killed."

"The rules."

"Yes. No contact with anyone from your former life. Not friends, not family outside of those who are moved with you, not colleagues from work. No one."

"I'm a scientific researcher. I publish several times a year..."

"That will have to stop."

Martinez's face contorted.

Colin had sat here before, watched other men wrestle with the decision to give up everything in exchange for their safety. He didn't envy Martinez, and he didn't judge him his grief.

"I need to talk to my wife."

"Of course. Would you like me to get her now?"

He nodded.

Colin pushed back his heavy metal chair and stood up,

grabbing his coffee as he went. At the door, he stopped and turned back to the other man. "I'm sorry you have to make this decision, Mr. Martinez."

Colin walked down a corridor, crumpling his coffee cup as he went. His stomach burned from the brew and his morning's work. Cases like this were his undoing. Everything the Martinez family had worked to build was about to be abandoned, leaving only the people themselves to carry on. It was unfair. It was horrific. It was just another day at the office.

He had become a U.S. Marshal to make a difference, to be a champion for the innocent. The simple reality was far less heroic. Colin stepped into a waiting room and closed the door behind him. "Mrs. Martinez, your husband would like to see you."

She raised bloodshot eyes to his. "What happens if Javier doesn't testify?"

He had been expecting the question. They always asked. He perched a hip on the table. "He'll be free to go back to his life."

"They'll leave us alone if he doesn't testify."

"They might." She was young, maybe late twenties. Too young to walk away from her mother and father, to have her children grow up without grandparents. "But the man who took a picture of your little girls getting off the school bus still knows where you live, still knows their names and what they look like. Are you comfortable with that?"

Her bottom lip quivered as she spoke. "I haven't been comfortable with anything since my husband watched that man on the subway get shot to death."

"Mrs. Martinez, I wish I could undo what's been done already, but I can't. All I can do is offer you and your family a way through this."

"We'll lose everything."

"You'll have a fresh start."

She put the back of her hand to her lips. "Officer..."

"Deputy Mitchell."

"Deputy Mitchell," she said, looking very serious, "what would you do if you were Javier?"

How he wished in that moment that he could wipe this away, make it as though it had never happened. What he was offering was the next best thing. "I would enter the program, Mrs. Martinez. I wouldn't be here if I didn't believe in it. WITSEC can give you a new life."

"I don't want a new life, I want my old one."

It pained him to say the words that needed to be said. "That's already gone."

~~~

Gwen walked into the sunroom carrying a painted wooden tray laden with two glasses of iced tea, a loaf of crusty herb bread, and butter. "I made the bread this morning with fresh thyme and rosemary from the garden."

"It looks fantastic."

"It does." She smiled at him, genuine affection lighting her face as she ripped a chunk off the loaf with her hands. She began to cover the steaming bread with butter, flashing Hank a conspiratorial wink. "One of my favorite vices. And how is your beautiful wife?"

"She's good." His flat mouth quirked with humor. "She's remodeling." Julie and Hank had just bought a new home in South Carolina.

"Oh, what fun! I adore home improvement projects. There's nothing like sculpting your environment, bringing your own sense of beauty into a space. It's art on a grand scale, don't you think?"

He looked around the room they were sitting in. It was narrow and tall, running the length of the farmhouse, with windows on three sides and old-fashioned pine wainscoting. The hardwood floor was wide-planked and scarred, with a time-honed honeyed finish.

A wicker cage chair hung from the ceiling in one corner, its bright yellow cushions coordinating with the rich paisley sofa on which he sat. A blue yoga mat lay unfurled in the middle of the floor, next to a wicker basket with a brass bell and a small book.

"I'm beginning to think so. Before we got married, I had a bunch of old furniture left from college that was all banged up. Julie gave it to Goodwill and bought brand new stuff that started out all banged up."

"Shabby chic."

He nodded. "That's what she said."

They smiled at each other.

"Why didn't Julie come with you?"

The bread in Hank's mouth turned suddenly thick. He worked to chew it as he reached for his drink. "She doesn't know I'm here."

Gwen leaned forward in her chair.

"I knew she'd want to come, and I needed to talk to you alone."

"What is it, Hank?"

He, Gwen, and Julie had been through a lot together in the last year, difficult times they might like to forget. Hank had been sent to investigate a murder and found a cryptic message with Julie's name. It turned out the message was meant for her to decode, and its secrets led them on an incredible journey.

Sweat broke out on his palms. "Do you remember, when Julie was trying to solve the cipher, I had my friend Chip run it through the computers at the NSA?"

"The man whose wife had the twins?"

"Yes."

She nodded. "I remember."

"Well, he didn't just run the cipher. He went looking for any references to the case at all. And he got a hit when he put in Julie's name and cross referenced it with McDowell."

"What did he find?"

"David Beaumont."

"David?" She sat upright. "My David?"

Hank nodded. "I didn't know why at first. And Julie was hurt, I was such a mess. I had to think about her."

"Of course you did."

"But afterward, I asked Chip to see what else he could find out. Why David Beaumont was listed in the NSA records at all."

"That doesn't make any sense. He was a composer."

"I know."

"But this is almost a year ago."

He nodded. "It took a long time to find the answer."

"And?"

"David Beaumont was in witness protection. He was listed

in the NSA Database because by marrying you, he was now associated with one of America's most wanted criminals, McDowell."

~~~

Colin was sitting at his desk doing paperwork when the thought of Gwen went through him in with a rush of heat. He lifted his pen and raised his head, exhaling like a man who'd been kicked in the stomach. Her remembered her scent, the breeze in her hair. Could feel her eyes on his, uneasy.

Sometimes he went weeks, or even months, without thinking of her this way. Then suddenly she'd be there, her presence as tangible to him as if she had been leaning over the desk.

Naked.

Not that Colin had ever seen Gwen naked, but he had pictured it more times than he could count. That woman excited him like no other ever had, and he'd never even touched her.

He had come close once, though.

Colin shook his head as if to clear it and turned to the clock. An hour past quitting time. He cleaned off his desk, then stood and pulled his suit coat over his dress shirt, flipping the collar down in one practiced motion.

There was no point in going home now. Already, his mind was shutting down all rational thought so he could wallow in memories of his dead friend's wife. Gwen's blue-gray eyes laughed at him in his mind, like a bride waiting to be taken to bed.

Bride. What the hell are you thinking?

He was saved from his own thoughts by the ringing of his cell phone. Glancing at the caller ID, he saw it was his brother, Rowan.

"How does he know?" Colin said to himself. He would swear, all he had to do was think of Gwen and his brother would come to her virtual rescue, more than fifteen years after the fact. The thought put him back in time, on the patio overlooking the river as he teetered on the edge of sanity itself. His body so close to Gwen's back, he could feel the heat of her along his entire torso like an intimate caress.

He reached up tentatively toward her arm, inching closer.

Colin had wanted this for so long, had wanted this woman since the moment he saw her. The fabric of her dress grazed his sensitive palm and his eyes closed in anticipation of the touch.

Rowan's voice behind him was fierce. "Colin!"

Colin had been so frustrated. Angry. He spent the rest of the evening drinking heavily and trying to catch Gwen's eye, until Rowan pulled him into a bedroom.

"What the hell are you doing?" asked Rowan, hands on his hips.

"None of your goddamn business," said Colin, aware of the slight slur in his speech.

"David's our friend, Gwen is his fiancé, and you are so far out of line it's not funny. That makes it my business."

Colin's ears started to ring. "They're engaged?"

Rowan nodded. "And you'd better not screw this up for David. Do you hear me?"

Indignation rose up inside him. "I wasn't the only one out on that veranda."

Rowan stepped closer. "You were the one whose hands were in the wrong place, brother."

"She wanted me to touch her."

"Bullshit."

"She did."

Rowan shook his head and ran his hand through his thick dark hair. "Did she say that?"

"Not exactly."

"Not exactly. What are you, a freakin' mind reader?"

Colin didn't answer, just stared at him.

"Fuck this." Rowan pulled his wallet out and shoved money at his brother. "I'm calling you a cab. Go to Dante's, or Michelle's, or whatever. But you can't stay here."

"I'm not going anywhere."

Rowan pointed his finger at Colin's chest. "You are, if I have to throw your ass in the cab myself."

Colin got in Rowan's face. Colin was bigger across the shoulders, stronger any day of the week. "You and what army?"

David stepped into the open doorway. "This army," he said quietly.

Colin stared at David, as much a brother to him as Rowan ever was. Colin had known him for as long as he could remember, had lived with him for more than ten years after David's father went away, loved him like family. Colin swallowed against the knot in his throat.

Gwen was a fantasy, the woman he wanted and could never have. David was so much more. Colin looked at the floor, raising his hands in surrender as the room pitched violently to one side. "Okay. I'll go."

It was the last time he ever saw David.

Colin's phone continued to ring, pulling him out of reverie. "Hey, Rowan," he answered. "What's up?"

~~~

Gwen's lower lip hung open. "Witness protection? Are you sure?"

"Yes."

"But why? What for?"

"I don't know. Chip tried to find out, but all the records are erased, every track covered."

"Well, someone must know for sure."

"The U.S. Marshal's office is responsible for changing the identity of witnesses."

Gwen's stomach took a dive, making her instantly nauseated.

Colin is a U.S. Marshal.

Hank was unaware of her distress. "The only way to find out would be to go through them. Maybe as David's widow you can get them to reopen the case."

Gwen was hot, dizzy with the implications of his words. Hadn't she known this day would come? A reckoning of sorts, an obligatory meeting with the man who had caused her eye to stray so long ago? Gwen believed in fate, and had suspected for some time that her path would cross Colin's again, forcing her to face her feelings for the man.

"Reopen the case?" she repeated, not understanding.

"The investigation into David's death."

She blinked her eyes, waiting for the words to make sense. "You think he was murdered?" It was hard to say the words, no less believe them. "The coroner did an autopsy. It was an accident."

"How can you be sure?"

"I was there, Hank," she said, holding her arms to her chest. "I went down with him the first few runs, then I went to the lodge to wait for him. It was only fifteen minutes or so before the paramedics came blazing by, and I knew something was wrong." She remembered the scene in great detail, the pitch of the sirens, the frantic energy that followed them up the mountain.

"Did you see anything unusual?"

"No," she said quickly, bowing her head. Just as fast it snapped back up again. "Wait, there was a man, a man in a big red parka. Someone David recognized. I didn't think anything of it at the time, but now...David said it was someone he knew a long time ago. Oh, my God, Hank," she whispered, her eyes wide with terror. "Do you think he killed David?"

~~~

Bright winter sunshine reflected off the snow, the landscape dotted with skiers in bold colored jackets and hats. It was a beautiful day for skiing, warmer than usual with only the slightest breeze.

Gwen stood to the side of the ski lift, waiting for David to finish his run. She enjoyed skiing, spending time outdoors and the sway of her body over the earth, but her husband was the real skier, slicing down trails with well-practiced accuracy and speed. He had taken a more challenging trail, while Gwen chose to stick with something simpler.

She saw his neon blue parka coming down the hill, watching as he sank into a crouch to gain speed, then turning into a wide arc, his skis throwing snow high into the air.

He caught up to her, his smile radiant. "Did you have a good run?" he asked.

"I hit some ice up on top, but the rest was powder."

"Mine was a little dicey, too." He put his arm around her and squeezed. "I'll ski with you this time."

Gwen smiled at her husband, so grateful she had this man to love above all others. David was her lover and her confidant, the one she looked for when she wanted to share her view of the world. "I'd like that," she said.

They took the ski lift back to the top of the mountain, the view a spectacular treat in itself. The rugged Vermont terrain was a mixture of tall mountains and deep valleys, everything covered in white and tinted varying shades of blue in the distance.

David was quiet on the way up the mountain, a far-away look in his eye. He'd been more reserved than normal for the last week or so, and Gwen was beginning to get concerned. "Is everything okay? It seems like something's bothering you."

He leaned back and lifted his arm for her to sit by his side. "The chase scene from that new film is driving me crazy. I can't seem to get the drum section right." He sighed. "And I've been thinking about my mother lately."

His mom had been killed when David was only six, the victim of a burglary gone wrong at the beauty shop where she worked. The family had been rocked to their core, David's dad packing up his young son and promptly moving to a new town that didn't hold such horrific memories.

"When I was in New York last week," said David, "I took the train up to Connecticut to visit her grave."

"Why didn't you tell me? I would have gone with you."

He shook his head. "I didn't have anything new to say, and I needed to go alone. It's a part of me that's always going to be a little raw."

"I'm sorry, David." She hugged him tightly. "Sorry you have to go through this."

The ski lift crested the mountain and they approached the exit ramp. The pair slid off the chair with practiced ease, and they turned toward the trail Gwen just completed, nearly bumping into a big man in a red parka. David stopped moving, staring into the goggles of the other man.

"Michael?" asked David.

"No," said the man, sidestepping the pair and skiing away. David continued to look after him as if he had seen a ghost.

"He looks just like someone I went to school with."

"From Vassar?"

"No. Not from Vassar." He shook he head. "Before that."

"They say everyone has a twin."

David stared after the man for several seconds before turned to his wife. "That must be it. Are you ready?"

"I am."

"Good. Let's rock this bunny slope, beautiful."

Chapter 3

The screen door slammed behind her as Gwen walked outside, noting the rain clouds that threatened on the horizon. The warmth of the day was still evident, though the sunshine had been replaced by overcast skies and an eerie pink glow over the landscape. Hank had left an hour earlier, the remaining loaf of herb bread tucked in a brown bag for the trip.

Needing to get a handle on her own emotions, Gwen had tried to meditate, sitting on the yoga mat in the sunroom and ringing the brass bell in an attempt to focus her thoughts. But the news of the day was her undoing, disrupting her natural rhythms, forcing her to leave her house to find the solace she craved.

The graveyard had been on the land since the seventeen hundreds, its early occupants unknown to Gwen except by their names, now barely visible on the weathered stones that marked them. It had seemed only right that her husband be buried here, closest to the person who had loved him best. Gwen rarely visited the cemetery, believing that her husband was neither there nor gone, but a part of the greater universe that surrounded her every day.

She unlatched a wrought iron gate and walked into the cemetery, nodding to the two tallest grave markers as she did. "Hello, Lucy, Caleb." A small wooden bench sat beneath a tall maple tree, and Gwen sat on it, resting her arm along the back and turning to where she knew a small metal plaque was tucked deep in the overgrown grass. "David."

Had he been brought to his eternal rest prematurely, by someone who meant to do him harm? Gwen pictured what she could remember of the man in red from the ski resort, which was very little. Had a childhood acquaintance killed her husband? After her initial memory, Gwen quickly realized she couldn't be sure of anything. She needed to know more about David and the witness protection program, information available only to the U.S. Marshal's Office.

Rowan had been so proud when Colin was accepted into the

prestigious program. Even David had been excited. Her husband's reaction made more sense now that she knew his own family had been relocated.

"What should I do?" she asked into the air, which had begun to pick up speed in anticipation of the coming storm. The answering silence was pronounced, and she felt tears wet her eyes, fresh grief for the man she could no longer talk to. Mourning her husband's death twelve years earlier had been the most difficult thing Gwen had ever done, and she didn't want to go back there, didn't want to feel what it was like to lose him all over again.

She had been a young bride, a seemingly younger widow. David had been seven years her senior. At thirty-six, Gwen had already experienced more of love and loss than some people see in seventy years.

Murdered. Was it possible? Could it be that she had been so close to evil, that it had reached into her life and taken her greatest love?

She wept harder, grief spilling out onto her cheeks as the wind carried away her cries.

When she was able, she wiped her face with the back of her hand, lifting her head to the swirling gray sky. "David, you deserve to have your murderer put away and punished for what he did." Her voice grew quiet. "But I don't want to do this. Forgive me, but I don't want to do this. Please..." she begged, her voice trailing off as the first drops of rain began to fall on her bare arms.

Her head dropped to her chest as the rain picked up speed, falling in fat drops, cooling her heated skin. She allowed it to overtake her, soaking her shirt and shorts, small rivers trailing down her legs and onto her sandaled feet before disappearing into the earth.

She breathed in the tangy air and allowed her mind to empty of the fear, the wishing for something different. The sound of the rainfall filled her head as she lifted her face to the sky. Poised before the universe, Gwen asked for the guidance she would need to complete this journey.

The kind eyes of Colin Mitchell appeared in her mind, clear

as a photograph, making her wince. She could see David's
reaction when Rowan had shared the news, his eyes wide with
wonder. *A Deputy with the U.S. Marshal's Office. Can you
believe that, Gwen?*

Everything was clear.

Gwen sat in the rain, letting the droplets water her spirit like
they were watering the earth around her. Time passed and the
tempo of the rain began to slow. Gwen opened her eyes, noting
the sun already peaking through a hole in the clouds.

A robin landed on the bench next to her, its feathers lit by
sunshine. "Looks like I'm going to Cold Spring," she said to the
animal, which cocked its head to the side and looked at her. "The
Hudson Valley in summer." She had always loved that area, had
missed it like she'd been born there, though she never expected
to be going back.

Standing, she walked several steps to David's marker,
kneeling in the wet grass and kissing her palm before pressing it
to the raised metal letters. "Anything for you, my love." She
stood, mentally calculating the time it would take her to drive to
the train station in Albany. "Anything at all."

~~~

When Colin left the office, he'd gone to the gym and picked
up two games of racquetball in an attempt to exorcise the Ghost
of Gwen. When that didn't work, he bought a six-pack of Stella
Artois and had himself a private party out on the veranda,
watching the Friday night boat traffic glide across the river and
wondering what might have happened if he'd confronted that
woman all those years ago.

It was a pastime he rarely allowed himself, thinking about
Gwen. He preferred to live his life in the here and now, with real
live women who existed right in front of him and didn't make
him feel like half of some mystic puzzle they had no intention of
putting together.

Colin stood at the kitchen sink, washing out the tall pilsner
glass that had been his weapon of choice last night. Only in the
last few hours was he starting to feel better, the emotions that
had come to a boil now cool and relenting.

It was time to get over Gwen Trueblood.

Maybe he should think about settling down, finding a woman to love and get married. Since Rowan married Tamra and had the baby, he was feeling decidedly envious. There was something nice about being part of a couple, having a family of your own. He turned around and took in the kitchen of his grandmother's house where he had lived alone for the better part of a decade.

He wasn't lonely, exactly. He just wanted something better, even if he couldn't imagine having those things with anyone other than Gwen. He cursed out loud at the direction his thoughts were taking again.

Colin stepped into the garage and reached for his bike helmet. A ride would clear his head, exhaust his body, give him some focus. God knows he could use some focus right now.

He clipped his bike shoes onto the pedals and fastened his helmet. His old Miyata had thousands of miles on it, its sleek steel frame as solid as the day it was built. How many of those miles had been spent thinking about Gwen?

A train whistled in the distance, but Colin paid no mind. He was already absorbed in his riding, the feel of the pavement beneath the narrow wheels, the breeze on his face. He imagined a life without Gwen in it, without heartache and disappointment, without a standard for all other women to be held to, and fall short of. And for a short while as he rode, Colin was happy.

~~~

Gwen stepped off the train, her cork wedge sandal landing squarely on the concrete platform. The sun shone in her eyes and she pulled her sunglasses down from their perch atop her head, unsticking one long blond curl as she walked. Her long sundress had three wide bands in the colors of frozen sherbet, its light fabric revealing her graceful neck before it draped snugly across her breasts.

Colin's home was a short walk from the station, nestled in a small clearing of trees across the tracks, but Gwen headed in the opposite direction. She sought out the waters of the Hudson River with a thirst in her soul that needing quenching.

A path emerged from the parking lot and she took it, a smile on her lips as she followed a curving route of stepping-stones over a rise, and the view before her opened to expose the deep greens of the dramatic river valley. Sharply rolling hills rose along the opposite bank, their tree-covered surface lush and inviting.

Gwen's feet stilled and she closed her eyes, taking a great breath into her lungs as she soaked up the heady scents of water and earth that surrounded her.

It was just as she remembered.

She exhaled in a trailing breath, opening her eyes to a ghost, standing before her in her memory. An impossibly young David stood in green shorts and a sun-kissed tan, beckoning her to follow. His image faded as quickly as it had appeared, and Gwen began to move, her footfalls on the familiar path seeming to erase the time since her last visit to this enchanted place.

The Chapel Restoration came into view and she giggled in anticipation.

How many times had she been here? The first was for Verdi, of that she was sure. A new Italian tenor, whose name escaped her now, who went on to become quite famous. He had sung the lush aria with the muscular skill of a well-trained voice, bringing Gwen to joyful tears.

She had wandered off from Rowan's party, leaving David playing cards with his friends as she explored. She'd been drawn first to the water, then to the music floating on the humid night air, calling her to sit and listen on the porch of the Chapel, its great round pillars framing doors left generously open to the summer night beyond. Gwen climbed the stone steps now, flanked on either side by the Chapel's cobblestone foundation, remembering that first evening that had drawn her to this perfect sanctuary.

The Chapel had once been a Catholic Church, though its Greek Revival architecture looked more like a tiny Parthenon than any cathedral Gwen had ever seen. Rowan had explained how it had been abandoned and brought back to life, now serving as an ecumenical chapel and performance center during the summer months.

She had always been able to feel God here, as if the universe had focused its energy on the small rectangular structure like a child collecting the sun's rays with a magnifying glass.

Gwen pulled at the door of the chapel, sharply disappointed to find it locked. Reaching up with her hand, she ran her fingers along the white painted surface, feeling the layers of paint and the texture of the wood beneath. How many layers since she'd been here last?

A guitarist playing Chopin.

A poetry reading, snuggled on a wooden pew with David.

"May I help you?"

Gwen jumped, turning to find a young pregnant woman in jeans and a t-shirt eying her strangely. "Oh, you gave me a start!" Gwen said, resting her hand on her chest as she began to laugh. "I was just thinking, 'If these walls could talk,' and then they did!"

The woman dropped her shoulders and took out a large key ring. "Sorry about that, I didn't mean to scare you."

"It's okay. Are you going inside?"

"I am. I work here." A mop and broom were tucked under her arm. "But the Chapel's closed to the public, except for scheduled events. There's a listing of programs online."

Gwen nodded, stepping back. "I understand, of course. You can't let every crazy ninny who shows up on the porch inside for a look-see." She smiled wide, staring at the girl, looking every bit the crazy and at least somewhat the ninny.

The girl tilted her head. "It used to be open all the time, but with the vandalism..."

"It's been vandalized?"

She nodded. "I have to do a graffiti check of the outside of the Chapel every week, along with the boulders on the bluff."

The building was situated some twenty feet from the water, which dropped down fifteen feet in a small cliff. Gwen had been down there numerous times, and knew the spot the woman was referring to. "Oh my, in your condition those rocks could be treacherous. Let me help you."

The woman's eyes lit momentarily before she shrugged off the suggestion. "That's all right, I can do it."

"Please, I insist," said Gwen, giving the girl's upper arm a light squeeze before turning on her heel. "I'll go check now, you just get started inside and I'll be right back to let you know if I found anything." Gwen strode to the shore and made her way down the cliff to the beach. Covered in small rocks and gravel, the area was clean except for a small collection of beer bottles, which she took with her back to the lawn and deposited next to the steps. Vandals were one thing, but Gwen could understand the desire to congregate at such a glorious spot and share a beer with friends. Hadn't she done as much with David and Rowan?

She walked back to the door of the Chapel, peeking in and seeing the girl tuck a strand of wayward hair behind her ear as she worked to polish the pews. What must it be like to be pregnant, to feel a life growing inside your womb? At one time in her life, Gwen thought motherhood would be a given for her, but she was no longer quite so certain.

"All I found were some empty beverage containers. I put them on the steps."

"Thank you." She put one hand on her hip and bit her lip. "Do you want to come in?"

"I do," said Gwen dramatically, "but I don't want to get you in trouble." She winked.

"It's all right, you can come in. I'm Crystal," she said, extending her hand.

Gwen shook it, taking in the tired look on the beautiful young woman's face. She couldn't be more than twenty and clearly becoming uncomfortable in her pregnancy. "I'm Gwen. Congratulations on the little one."

"Thanks," Crystal said, her face brightening as she raised a hand to her protruding belly. "Can you believe I'm got another month left? I don't think I'm going to make it."

"How exciting!" Gwen walked around the edge of the space, her hand trailing along the pews as memories from her youth came flooding through her mind.

"Me and Danny," said Crystal, "are getting married in the Chapel this fall."

"Oh, how lovely!" Gwen sighed, imaging the young Crystal as a bride. "I've always loved it here. You're a very lucky lady to be beginning a marriage within such hallowed walls."

"You've been here before?"

"Many times, years ago," she said, waving her hands. "Before my husband and I were married, we used to come up from the city to visit a friend right across the tracks."

Crystal's brow furrowed. "Who?"

"Rowan Mitchell."

"I know Rowan. His grandmother was the school librarian at the high school when I was there. She was a nice lady. Do you know her, too?"

Gwen shook her head. "She was never home when I was here. I understand she was quite the world traveler."

Crystal nodded. "She used to bring souvenirs into school, to show students from her trips."

"Indeed, the house was filled with them."

"Are you going to see Rowan today?"

"No, his brother Colin."

"Colin doesn't live here anymore. He married an Italian woman a few years ago and moved over there. They have a son, I think."

Gwen's face fell, her eyes wide. A stinging sensation splashed into her abdomen. *A son. Colin is married with a son.*

She chastised herself for feeling betrayed. What business was it of hers if Colin Mitchell got married? She had never given the man any reason to believe she was interested in him. She wasn't interested in him. Heavens, she hadn't even seen him in more than ten years. A picture of Colin with his young bride and baby appeared in her mind, and she bristled at the thought.

"I'm sorry you didn't know," Crystal said quietly, "but Rowan must know where Colin is. Maybe he could put you in touch. Was it important?"

Honest to a fault, Gwen considered telling Crystal the truth, but she could imagine the young woman's response. *Murder. Witness protection.*

"I just wanted to catch up with an old friend." She stood up, decided. "I'm going to stop by and pay Rowan a visit while I'm in town. He was a good friend to my husband, and I've let too many years go by without stopping to say hello. It was very nice speaking with you, Crystal. I appreciate you letting me inside."

"You're very welcome. The Chapel was meant for everyone,

don't you think?"

"I do, Crystal. I do."

Chapter 4

She made her way back through to the train station parking lot, carefully crossing the tracks and disappearing into the woods like a child. Despite the time that had passed since her last foray through these trees, Gwen knew she could find the house with her eyes closed.

Set back some two hundred feet from the river on a small hill, the Mitchell home stood separate from the more modern developments that had sprung up since it was built at the turn of the century by Colin's great grandfather, a retired shipping captain. It was a unique home with a four-story round turret that was part of the lower two floors, and extended beyond them like a lighthouse. The front of the house faced the water, a wide veranda reaching toward the lustrous river below.

A winding driveway connected the house to the street, but this direct route through the forest was the path she had always taken with David. Ducking under the branch of an oak tree, Gwen enjoyed the intimacy of her backwoods approach, feeling like a child crossing the backyards of her neighbors to visit an old friend.

Rowan Mitchell. She smiled at the name. Her husband's best friend, Rowan and David had been inseparable until life took them in different directions. David became a musician, primarily working in New York City, then a composer of soundtracks for theater and film, while Rowan took over the business world. The last Gwen knew, Rowan was the Chief Financial Officer for one of the largest publishing houses in the world, living and working somewhere in California. He'd been David's best man at their wedding.

The house came into view, its pale green exterior shining in pleasant contrast to its darker green surroundings. A large weeping willow graced the west side of the property, its branches waiting to shade the veranda between the house and its million-dollar view. Stone steps extended from a lower lawn up to the house proper, edged with a grand scale garden of rhododendrons and small round azaleas.

The flowers were new and lovely, showing an awareness of form that Gwen's artist's eye could appreciate. She struggled to reconcile the obvious talent of the gardener with the businesslike image she held of Rowan, and decided he must have hired someone to care for the property.

Gwen's feather-light touch graced the bold magenta of the rhododendron as she swayed up the steps, their fruity scent reaching her nostrils in abundance. She inhaled deeply into her lungs, releasing the disappointment of the day, and worked to open her mind to new possibilities.

~~~

A movement in the distant yard caught his eye and he squinted, trying to make out whomever had wandered onto his property. It wasn't unheard of for an interloper to appear, with the house so close to the train station and the Chapel Restoration. Rowan had several times suggested their grandmother fence in the land, but she had refused, saying she would miss the deer and other wildlife making their way to the river.

It was a woman, blond with a bright orange dress. She moved with a casual grace that was vaguely familiar, heading directly for the stairs that rose to the lawn and veranda.

Colin turned off the tap and leaned toward the window.

Gwen.

The word was a breathless wish, an aching curse. His heart lurched, even as reason slammed down on his thoughts with a heavy foot. He turned away from the window and spun in a circle.

He lifted his head to the window again, expecting not to see whatever had reminded him of Gwen and froze, his mouth falling open. She stopped to smell a bright purple blossom next to the stone staircase, her eyes closing and a smile spreading across her lips.

His body clenched, blood pumping. He knew her like he knew his own reflection. Had seen her countless times in dreams, in waking awareness so keen he would swear she must be feeling it right then, too.

Sweat broke out on his hands as he clenched and opened

them. He walked to the door and stepped outside just as she stepped onto the veranda, their eyes meeting across the small space.

"Gwen," he said, his voice husky and bare. He lifted his arms ever so slightly, opening to her in invitation, watching her face as she wavered before closing the distance and settling against his chest.

He was on fire, her unique scent encompassing him as he held her. A long curly lock of her hair stuck to the stubble on his cheek.

"I've missed you," she whispered, and his heart swelled. She had come to him. After so much time, so many rebuffs, Gwen Trueblood was finally back where she belonged.

~~~

Gwen reveled in the feel of his muscled torso against her softness, the strength of his solid arm holding her to him. Lust came quickly, and she daringly welcomed it like a hand trailing behind a boat in the ocean. Deliberately she leaned into him, her hand trailing up his bicep to rest at the base of his neck, grazing the bare skin there with the lightest of touches.

She knew she stood at the threshold of something she could not rescind. Colin had always been her downfall, her temptation, her weakness. His spirit was as familiar to her as the scent of her own home, and she rejoiced in seeing him again, even knowing as she did so that it was like playing with a deadly snake. You could only do so for so long before it would strike you.

They stood in the summer sunshine in this place of her youth, their bodies gently swaying. Gwen heard the low moan of attraction deep in his throat, and battled the urge to return it. It would be so easy to turn in his arms and bring her mouth to his. With more strength than she knew she possessed, she lifted her head and smiled at him casually.

"Hello, Colin."

His voice was intimate and deep. "Hey there."

She lowered her arms and stepped back. "You weren't supposed to be here."

"What do you mean?"

"I heard you were living in Italy, married with a young son."

"Rowan's living in Italy, married with a young son."

She smiled wide, showing her teeth. "Ah. But not you."

"Nope. I'm right here. Same place I've been since the last time you saw me."

The words strummed through her head like a chord, and she caught herself. She wasn't interested in Colin. It was just exciting to feel something—anything—for a man.

He reached down and took her hand in his, leading her to a seating area. "I wondered if I would see you again."

"Yes," she said, sitting down on a wrought iron loveseat with a plush yellow cushion. "I wondered that, too."

"How've you been?"

"Good. Still in Vermont. Still in the same house." Of course, Colin hadn't been there. He'd been absent from their lives since the day the two of them had stood in this very spot, nearly touching in the warm evening's breeze.

If Rowan hadn't come along...

She stopped her thoughts from going down that path. She focused instead on memories of Rowan, such a good friend to her David through the years. He had stayed in touch when they moved to Vermont, visited them every fall before David died. He hadn't left her side at the funeral, when she had so desperately needed his strength.

David's father had passed away when he was in middle school. There was no other family, and Rowan had asked his grandmother if his best friend might have a home with them. The way David told it, Dottie Mitchell never even considered saying no. Rowan and David's friendship had grown to include the younger Colin, and the three became close as family.

Until I came along.

She thought she had let go of the guilt, but sitting here with the man who had paid the biggest price for her transgression, she was acutely aware she had not.

She met his eyes, seeing myriad emotions reflected in their golden brown depths. "I'm sorry, Colin."

"What for?"

"Everything. That you and David weren't close in the years before his death."

He stared at her for some time without speaking, then nodded. "That wasn't your fault. I did miss him though. I missed you both."

"It was David I came to talk to you about." She tucked a wayward curl behind her ear, words rushing to her mouth before she considered their import. "Why didn't you come to the funeral?" It wasn't what she'd planned to say. She had no intention of broaching the subject, but there it was, begging for her attention. "It hurt me, Colin. It hurt Rowan."

He stood up, shoving his hands in his pockets and turning away from her. He stared at the horizon for minutes without answering.

Gwen leaned back into her seat and let her eyes fall to the river. So many things hung between her and Colin. So many words unsaid, so many thoughts unspoken.

David, forgive me for coming here. She opened her eyes, shaking her head at her own ridiculous thoughts.

"Do you want a glass of wine?" he asked, ignoring her question.

She nodded and watched as he went inside. From the warm glow of the kitchen window, she watched him remove the cork with punishing movements, the muscles of his forearm standing out against his skin.

Mercy, that man is sexy.

He walked back outside and handed her a glass of something dark and spicy.

"I was at David's funeral."

She tilted her head and eyed him curiously.

"I was there, Gwen. He's buried in the garden at your home, with the little black gate around it."

She couldn't have been more shocked. "Why didn't I see you?"

"I hung back."

"Why?"

His mouth remained closed, his lips pursed, then relaxed. "I was there on official business."

A stillness overtook them both as they stared into each other's eyes.

"Then it's true. David was in witness protection."

He nodded. "How did you find out?"

"I was told by a friend," she said, her tone implying he wasn't much of one for keeping it from her. "He was concerned that David's death might not have been accidental. I came here to find out what you know about David's past, if anyone might have wanted to hurt him."

"I've sworn an oath, Gwen. One that I take very seriously."

"I need the truth, Colin." She walked toward him, her eyes pleading. "You're the only one who can tell me what I need to know."

He cursed under his breath. "It's not that easy, Gwen."

"Don't make me beg." She stepped closer to him. "You're going to tell me. I can see it on your face, I can see it the way you're holding yourself," she said, her eyes roaming the length of him. She was angry that he was toying with her, keeping the information she so desperately wanted to know.

He grabbed her wrist and met her stare, his eyes mirroring her anger. "You can feel it, Gwen. Just say it. You know I'm going to tell you because you can feel it in your bones, just like you've been able to feel me since that day on the train."

In her mind she was in the train car, the seat swaying beneath her semi-sleeping form as she reveled in the fantasy of making love to this man. Embarrassment and lust mingled, flushing her cheeks with heat.

Not a fantasy at all.

"Stop," she whispered.

His stare dropped to her lips. "No," he said firmly. "Not this time, Gwen." He dropped his head and took her mouth in a kiss of determined pleasure. The intensity of it wiped rational thought from her brain, leaving only her animal self to respond to his lips on hers, his body pressed against her in a crushing embrace.

Chapter 5

"Stop it. Colin, please." He could hear the emotion in her voice, knew she was close to tears. He begrudgingly released her, cool air rushing in when she took a step back.

Damn, she is beautiful.

Dusk had settled in, her patrician features lit by the light spilling from the house. His body ached to rake her back into his arms, make her realize how good they could be together. He'd finally had a taste of her, and the thirst that had plagued him for years was now a raging need for the river that was Gwen.

She crossed her arms over her chest and turned away from him. His muscles itched to follow her, turn her back around, rewind time and get back to the moment when they first connected, the electric energy that went straight from her mouth to his very core.

Gwen walked back to the loveseat and picked up her wine. "Tell me, Colin. Tell me why he was in WITSEC."

She was asking too much, the only thing he couldn't reveal. It went against everything he believed in, everything that kept people safe.

David's already dead. You can't save him now.

"David's father was placed in the program when David was six."

"His father?"

Colin nodded. "He testified against his cronies in exchange for his freedom. The family was placed in Connecticut initially, but David's mother just couldn't keep herself from calling her mother to wish her a happy birthday."

"Oh, my God." Gwen covered her mouth with her hands.

"She was gunned down in a beauty shop outside of Hartford. The local cops did a phenomenal job of getting David and his father to safety quickly."

"How did they know?"

"We notify the local authorities when a witness is placed in their jurisdiction. A lot of these people are criminals, and a lot of criminals have a penchant for illegal activity. It helps to have the cops keeping an eye on things."

Gwen's bottom lip fell. "Is that what happened to his father, too? Was he killed?"

Colin sat down. "No. He went to prison."

She was confused. "He died in prison?"

"He didn't die at all."

"But, that's why David came to live with you and Rowan!"

"No. David came to live with us when his father went to jail. It was his idea to say his father was dead. He was ashamed. He wanted a fresh start with our family. He even went so far as to have my grandmother put a grave stone in the local cemetery."

"That's awful."

"Jerry ruined David's life once. David didn't want him to be able to do it again. He blamed his dad for his mother's death. She was unhappy."

"How did you find out he was in WITSEC?"

"He broke down and told Rowan the truth the first time he got drunk in Eddie Mangione's tree house."

She smiled. "I've heard a lot of stories about that tree house."

"David couldn't handle the lies. A lot of kids can't, it's just too much for them."

"I can only imagine."

"When David found out he was going to have to move again, the three of us hatched a plan to get him to stay. He told my grandmother the truth, and she couldn't bear to send him off to God-knows where."

"That was very kind of her."

He nodded. "Grams loved David."

"We all did."

"He's the reason I wanted to become a U.S. Marshal, you know. I wanted to help people like him."

"That's very noble of you."

He looked off to the side. "The idea was noble. The reality isn't quite so honorable. I spend my days getting health club memberships for people named Benny the Bull."

"And their families."

He nodded. "And their families."

Gwen sipped her wine. "All these years, I thought my father-in-law was dead. I've never even met him. Do you know where he is now?"

"No. He was released from prison six weeks before David died, and never reentered the program."

"Six weeks!"

"Yes, why?"

Gwen put her drink down on the glass table with a clink. "I believe David may have been murdered."

Colin shook his head. "I investigated that possibility while I was in Vermont for the funeral. That was what I was sent there to do. I talked to the coroner, the sheriff. It was an accident, Gwen. The slopes were icy."

"That day on the mountain, just before he died, David saw someone he recognized from school."

Colin slammed his drink down. "What? Are you sure?"

"Yes. I was standing right next to him. He was a big man in a red ski parka and goggles. David called him Michael."

"Can you identify him?"

She shook her head. "Not with the goggles on. David saw his face, not me."

"Why didn't you say something sooner?"

"I thought I did mention it, actually. But I didn't know David was in WITSEC, Colin. I had no reason to think anything of it at the time."

"That's true. I'm sorry, I wasn't thinking." Colin ran his hand through his hair. "I screwed up. I should have talked to you myself."

"You were there?"

"I came as soon as I heard. But I let the local cops interview you. I didn't want you to know I was there."

"Sheriff McDonald?"

"Yes, why?"

Gwen looked down into her glass of wine, her brows drawn together. "I might be wrong about this, Colin, but I think I told McDonald about Michael."

"What?"

She nodded. "I think so." She shook her head. "But I was a disaster. It's hard to be sure of anything."

~~~

Colin walked toward the trees in the light of the full moon, an hour after Gwen went to bed. He could hardly believe she was sleeping under his roof, having reappeared in his life so unexpectedly. He ducked under the boughs of the majestic old pines that separated his home from the train station and made his way to the river.

It was deeply troubling to consider the possibility that David was murdered. It had been Colin's investigation, his responsibility. He cursed himself as he made his way past the boulders at the Chapel Restoration, down the bank, and settled his body on a large rock. If he bungled that investigation, it was because of his feelings for Gwen, not wanting to interview her personally and see her pain.

He thought he could trust the sheriff to ask a few questions, never considering the other man might be part of a larger conspiracy. In fact, Colin had never really considered foul play. He admitted to himself that he had asked for the assignment only to attend services for his friend who had died and maybe to get a glimpse of Gwen. The investigation aspect was an afterthought, a procedural requirement, a bunch of paperwork he didn't take too seriously.

And David's murderer had walked away, because of his carelessness.

Colin lifted his head to the sky, taking in the twinkling stars above him. He didn't know if his friend could hear him, didn't know exactly what he believed about death. "I'm sorry, David," he said, his voice cracking. "I should have done better." A boat slipped past in the distance, its green and white lights glowing brightly. "I promise you, I'll find out who did this, make them pay for what they did. They won't get away from me again."

Chapter 6

Restless dreams plagued Gwen as she slept. She imagined she snuggled closer to the heat of David's body, resting her head on his shoulder. She felt his arm lightly tracing a path from her lower back up to her shoulder blade and moaned in satisfaction.

"You awake?" he asked, and she nodded. He shifted to face her, running his hand up her hip to her arm and shoulder. "I had a dream about you," he said.

She opened her eyes to stare into his, a slight smile curling one side of her mouth.

My David.

Relief flooded her senses at the sight of him, a gratefulness filling her heart at his presence. Why was that? Had he been away on a trip and only now returned? Was he out when she went to bed, only sneaking under the covers after she had fallen asleep?

I can't remember.

"What was your dream about?" she asked.

"We were on a train." As he said the words, they seemed to fly through the air, landing, fully clothed, on a commuter train. It was nighttime, and though Gwen could not see beyond the interior of the car, she knew it rumbled alongside the Hudson River. David was turned away from her, staring past the reflected interior of the train car to the hidden landscape beyond, and she felt very far away from him.

When he spoke, it was so quiet she could barely make out the words. "I would let you go, if that's what you wanted."

"Never," she whispered, upset that he would suggest such a thing.

David turned toward her, his eyes wet with unshed tears. "I saw you with him."

Colin.

Shame filled her gut, clawing at her. "I never did anything..." She shook her head.

"I saw you right here, on this train," he wept, "letting him touch you, letting him make love to you."

A loud feminine moan behind her made Gwen turn around. There, in the next seat over, was an image of herself astride Colin Mitchell's lap, wearing only a long set of golden beads, clothes hanging off her body. They were kissing passionately, their cheeks flushed, hands grabbing at each other as they rocked in an intimate dance. Gwen's stricken eyes met those of her twin, heavy-lidded with lust, as the image called out again, unashamed.

Gwen's throat worked, panic rising. "No, David, I didn't..."

"Do you love him, Gwen?"

Then she was the one with Colin, joined as lovers, so close to the edge she might explode, her eyes locked with the man beneath her. The feel of him was almost unbearable, the heat of his body and the slick stick of sweat between them indistinguishable from each other.

Colin fiercely pulled her body onto his, and she quivered. "Tell him, Gwen. Tell him you love me."

He moved beneath her and her eyes closed in surrender.

David's voice invaded her ears, whining, distracting her. "Do you love him?"

Her eyes flew open and she looked to him, the action returning her to his side, fully clothed. "I love you, David. Only you."

She was hot, her skin damp with sweat and her pulse pounding. Her body ached with sexual need.

David smiled. "I love you, too, honey." He kissed the top of her head and grasped her hand, turning back to his view of the darkness.

Gwen sat in stunned silence, afraid to see what might be beside her. Slowly, her head turned of its own accord.

A naked Colin stared at her with contempt. "You're a liar."

"I didn't lie," she said, somehow certain David could no longer hear her, even as she squeezed his hand. "I do love him, Colin. I'm sorry."

Colin stood, pulling on a pair of jeans with exacting movements. "I know you love your husband. That was never the issue. But you told him you loved only him, Gwen, and that," he said, buckling his belt, "is a goddamn lie."

Gwen awoke to a cool breeze across her skin, one leg hanging out of the covers and draped back over the fluffy bedding. Taking in the unfamiliar room, her stomach dipped as she remembered where she was, glimpses of the kiss she had shared with Colin haunting her memory.

Not a dream after all.

She groaned, sitting up in bed as she flung back the covers.

She was getting sidetracked. She came back here to find out who had murdered her husband, not to get involved with Colin Mitchell.

Well, then maybe you should keep your lips to yourself, Gwen.

Brushing her thick golden hair in the mirror, she nodded. "I will definitely be keeping my lips to myself today." She gave herself a wink and headed downstairs to set the record straight with Colin.

~~~

"So, you're not going to be kissing me today?" asked Colin, a light smile on his lips. Gwen had come downstairs determined to make him understand that their amorous exchange yesterday was a mistake, pure and simple.

"No. I shouldn't have been kissing you yesterday, but I hadn't seen you in so long..."

"Oh, is that why?"

She cocked her head to the side. "Maybe. I don't know." She crossed her arms over her chest. "It does sound a little silly when I say it out loud."

"No. It doesn't sound silly at all. But if I were you, I would skip my high school reunion."

She pursed her lips and gave him a look before taking the bold red mug of coffee he offered. "Good heavens, this is delicious." Gwen inhaled the rich scent of the steaming coffee. "What kind of beans do you use?"

"I grow them myself in a hothouse in the backyard."

She stared at him, dumbfounded. "You're pulling my leg."

He shook his head. "It's a lot of work, but it's worth it."

"I didn't even know that was possible. Where did you find a

coffee plant here in the States?"

"Interesting story. Six years ago, I was in Columbia on a case for several months. I met a woman there. Paola. She was young. Beautiful."

Gwen watched as Colin's face was transformed by the memory, a twinge of jealousy curling in her stomach.

"Her family owned a coffee farm in the mountains." He turned away, slowly pouring himself a cup. "She took me there once." He paused, and Gwen wondered what he was keeping to himself. "They were the most exquisite blue-green beans you've ever seen in your life."

"You must have cared for her."

He rested his open palm across his heart and nodded. "When it came time for me to leave," he looked down into his cup, "she gave me a coffee plant. A single plant in a pottery jar she'd made for me on her pottery wheel."

"Oh, Colin, what a touching story. And you've nurtured and tended to that plant ever since, harvesting and roasting your own beans in a greenhouse here in New York." She was in awe. This was a side of him she'd never seen before.

"It's a lot of work, but the orphans help."

"Orphans?"

He nodded. "A few years ago, I got dressed for golf and I caught sight of myself in the mirror. I was wearing a nice new polo shirt, which cost about a hundred bucks. For a polo shirt. All of a sudden, it just hit me. I have to give something back. You know?"

Gwen settled onto a barstool, her eyes wide. "I do."

"So I started an orphanage. There used to be loads of them," he said, gesturing with his hands. "You know, like in Little Orphan Annie."

Gwen began to squint at him.

"But no one opens up any orphanages anymore. Where are all those orphans supposed to go? There was a need, you know, a real need, so I decided to fill it."

"Where is the orphanage?" she asked, taking another sip of the delicious brew.

"Underground."

Coffee sprayed out of her mouth, covering the floor in a fine mist.

He leaned across the counter, putting his sincere face close to hers. "Of course. I had to hide them from the Bald Eagles I raise on the lawn. They're known for snatching small children, those damn eagles."

She couldn't help the grin that was tugging at the corners of her mouth. "Colin, where'd you get the coffee beans?"

He opened a cupboard and threw a small white bag to her. The label read COFFEE BEANS, MEDIUM ROAST, $3.99/lb.

Gwen laughed in spite of herself. "I'd forgotten what an ass you can be."

"You mean you'd forgotten how damn cute I can be." He winked, and her breath caught in her chest.

Yes, she thought to herself. *I'd forgotten that, too.*

"But don't even think about kissing me," he said, holding his hand up between them. "These lips are strictly off-limits."

"Oh, I wouldn't dream of it," she said, her mind suddenly flashing to her dream from the night before. She instantly felt her cheeks color, and worked to keep an innocent look on her face. "What time is your train?"

Colin was headed to his office in the city to gather what information he could from David's WITSEC file. He checked his watch. "Twenty minutes. If all goes well, I should be back around lunchtime."

Gwen nodded, a strange and troubling apprehension weighing on her thoughts. "God speed," she said sincerely, then added, "Be careful, Colin.

~~~

Graham Walker leaned back in his large leather desk chair. "Do you know what you're asking me to do?"

Colin felt like a teenager being chastised by his father. When Colin first joined the Marshal's Office, he was green, out to prove himself. It was Walker who had taken him under his wing, worked with him, taught him when to be eager and when to pipe down. The older man showed him how to build a new life for a witness, how to pick a suitable environment and make a person disappear like a rabbit from a hat.

The Southern District of New York branch of the U.S. Marshal's Office was predominantly concerned with security for court trials and the safeguarding of witnesses. Colin was one of only a handful of deputies who worked for the WITSEC division, and he reported directly to Walker, as he had for the last eight years.

The two of them shared a bond, an understanding of sorts. Colin would trust Walker with his life, and suspected his boss would do likewise.

"I'm asking you to help me," said Colin.

Walker raised his voice. "You're asking for a hell of a lot more than that, Mitchell." He stabbed his finger at Colin. "You're asking me to sacrifice my integrity."

Colin shook his head quickly. He had known it would be hard to come here and ask Walker for help. The man walked the straight and narrow, following procedure to the letter and insisting that those under his command follow his example. In his tenure as head of the division, Walker had cleaned out the ranks, getting rid of deputies who failed to meet his high standards, either by firing them or having them shipped to other offices.

"No, sir, I'm not. I'm asking you to give me access to the information I need to make sure justice was carried out. You of all people know how important it is to get it right." Colin pointed his thumb at his breastbone. "I'm the one who handled the review of Beaumont's death. If my determination that his death was accidental is wrong, then that's the right thing to do in this case."

"You're personally involved."

"Exactly. No one cares about this like case I do."

Walker lowered his voice, his deep baritone like the hum of a motor. "No one could screw it up like you could. You're too close to this one, Mitchell. You have to know when to step back."

"That's not what you said back then, Graham. You hand-picked me to go to Vermont and investigate."

"That was a mistake on my part." Walker leaned forward over his desk, his eyes never leaving Colin's. "You were distraught, demanding to be included in the investigation. Do you remember?"

An image flashed in Colin's memory--a younger version of himself breaking down in this very office upon learning of David's death.

Walker shook his head. "I let my concern for you as a friend impact my judgment. I knew it then, and I allowed it anyway. I'm not going to make the same mistake again, especially if there's reason to believe an error was made."

Colin dropped his head a fraction, steepling his hands. "You and I go back a long way, Graham."

"Don't pull this garbage with me, Mitchell."

"If I had to pick out one person from WITSEC who I knew had my back, it would be you."

"I'm not doing it."

"Hear me out. I have a relationship with the widow. She trusts me, and she doesn't trust anybody right now. All we have to go on is what she remembers from that day."

Walker leaned back in his chair. "I thought you were estranged from the family."

"Not anymore. She's staying at my house right now."

"I see," said Walker, pursing his lips as he stood up and turned to face the cityscape beyond. He sighed heavily. "This view comes with great responsibility."

"Yes."

"I won't be looking at it forever."

Colin considered his words. Graham was sixty-five, and rumors had begun circulating about his retirement.

"Sometimes I think I've been sitting in this office for too long. That I've lost touch with the people we work to protect," said Graham, shrugging his shoulders and turning back to Colin. "Your friend's father was my placement. I worked with the family, arranged for their credentials. What do you know about him?"

"Only what David told me. He was an accountant for organized crime who turned on his buddies."

Walker scoffed. "He was no accountant. They called him the dispatcher. When something—or someone—needed to be taken care of, it was Jerry who sent the muscle to take care of it."

Colin's eyes grew wide. "Jerry Ahearn?"

Walker nodded.

Ahearn was infamous in WITSEC history. His testimony resulted in the conviction of four of the biggest names in the history of organized crime. While Ahearn himself was associated with more than twenty murders, he had never been present at a crime scene, never been the trigger man.

Colin's voice was barely more than a whisper. "Jerry Ahearn was David Beaumont's father."

"David *Ahearn* and his mother Adele went into WITSEC with Jerry in 1975. Adele didn't make it six months before making contact with her family, which resulted in her quick and certain demise."

"I knew about the mom."

Walker nodded. "I was there. Overkill. It was a bloodbath." He turned back around to face Colin. "Adele was beautiful and sweet, a striking woman, a loving mother. There is no greater tragedy." A sad smile graced his lips.

Colin had heard stories from David about the countless days the boy and his mother spent on the slopes, how she helped him collect rocks in the summertime and leaves in the fall. He knew just how much the woman had been missed.

Walker pinched the bridge of his nose. "Sometimes you know when a person's going to crack, when they can't handle the pressure and follow the rules. But I didn't see that one coming at all." Sadness was plain on his features, and he made a rough sound in his throat. "I would have bet my last dollar that Adele would follow the straight and narrow, that she'd keep herself and her family safe no matter what."

"But she didn't."

"No. She didn't. Damn shame, too. I pulled Jerry and his boy out of Connecticut and relocated them to Cold Spring. Ahearn kept his nose clean for a while, then got busted for drug trafficking, leaving his son a ward of the state. If your grandmother hadn't stepped forward, he would have gone into foster care at that point."

"What does this have to do with reopening the investigation into David's death?"

"Jerry Ahearn came to see me when he got out of jail. He'd been incarcerated in a WITSEC prison unit, so he didn't mix with the general population. He wanted a fresh start, a new identity. He felt he'd been compromised, and your grandmother had already put on a funeral for Jerry Beaumont, complete with a headstone. It left him with few options."

"Why did he think his identity had been compromised?"

"He felt the local authorities in Cold Spring were out to get him. He even accused an officer there of setting up the whole sting that got him arrested, claiming he was framed."

"What officer?"

Walker shook his head, his gaze unfocused. "It was a long time ago, I don't remember the name. It would be in my notes in the file."

"Was there any truth to Jerry's suspicions?"

"Not as far as I could ascertain. I looked at the evidence and I believe he was guilty. I refused to provide him with another placement. He had valid credentials; he could go anywhere he wanted except home to Cold Spring."

"Do you know where he is now?"

"Not exactly."

Colin looked at him quizzically.

"John Campbell testified against the same crime ring a few years ago. He insisted Ahearn's back in the fold." Walker shrugged. "We don't have any direct evidence that supports that claim."

Stranger things had been known to happen, though if it was true, it was a wonder he survived long enough to ingratiate himself back with his cronies.

"I need to see if David was murdered," said Colin.

Walker nodded in resignation. "I know you do. What do you need from me?"

Chapter 7

Colin and Gwen were in Colin's dining room, the large rectangular table covered in stacks and piles of papers. "That's the last of the court transcripts," said Gwen, closing a binder and putting it aside.

"Find anything?"

"Three Michaels are mentioned. Michael Gallente was sentenced to three consecutive life terms based on Ahearn's testimony. Michael Hendrickson was one of the kills ordered by Ahearn in the year before he turned, and Michael Dobbs was one of the defense attorneys for Leveen."

Marc Leveen was the biggest fish Ahearn netted when he testified for the feds, and the second in command of the crime ring at the time. He was the enforcer, determining the punishments for infractions for the organization. Jerry Ahearn was Leveen's right-hand man, seeing that all of his boss's bidding went down smoothly.

"Doesn't sound like any of those could be our guy. Maybe a son with the same first name, but no direct link. I wish I knew where the hell Ahearn is. He's the one who could shed some light on who Michael might be."

"Your boss didn't know?"

He shrugged. "Walker heard Ahearn was back in Boston, up to his old tricks."

"I thought his old friends wanted him dead for testifying against their members."

"Things change. When Leveen went down there was a shift of power. Then Manning died of natural causes. Who knows who's in charge today, and how they feel about Jerry Ahearn?"

"That's true." She gestured to the papers in front of him. "Did you find anything?"

While Gwen had been going through court documents, Colin had been reading all the WITSEC files on Jerry Ahearn and his family. "One thing struck me as odd. Ahearn requested a placement in the southwest, not the northeast."

"He probably wanted to get as far away as possible."

Colin nodded. "I'm sure. But we try to honor requests like that. It doesn't make a difference to us one way or another."

"That is strange."

"And the coroner's report on Adele Ahearn shows she was almost two months pregnant when she was killed."

Gwen cringed. "Oh, that's awful." She pushed back her chair and stood. "I'm getting a glass of wine. Would you like one?"

"Yes, please." Colin picked up his phone. "I still haven't heard back from Officer McDonald in Vermont."

She spoke from the kitchen. "When did you call him?"

"On my way back from the city." He scrolled through his messages, finding nothing from the sheriff. "Did you know him?"

"Sort of. He was in office the whole time I lived there, and it's a small town. We nodded to each other on the street, that sort of thing." She handed Colin his wine.

"Did David know him?"

Gwen thought about that. "Yes, I suppose he did. I wouldn't say they were friends, but I did see them talking a time or two." She shimmied her shoulders. "Something about McDonald always rubbed me the wrong way."

"Like, how?"

"Oh, nothing horrible, I don't believe. I just chalked it up to him being a politician." In her mind's eye, Gwen could remember the sheriff and the cool exchanges he sometimes shared with her husband. "Did McDonald know David was in WITSEC?"

"He shouldn't have. The Cold Spring authorities would have been notified because of Jerry, but by the time David moved to Vermont his father was long gone."

Colin spoke. "I need to talk to Jerry," he said, letting his pen drop to his yellow lined legal pad.

"Do you think we can find him?"

"I think we're going to have to try."

Gwen nodded. "We'll leave in the morning?"

"I don't see why not."

~~~

"Keep your eye on the ball. Watch it hit the bat."

"I am."

"No, you swung and missed. Which is why I'm telling you this." Jason McDonald shook his head at his twelve year-old son, then wound up and pitched the ball up and away, just the way Garret liked them. Sure enough the boy went for it, the barrel of the bat hitting the ball with a metallic crack and propelling it deep into center field.

"Nice one." He looked at his son as he threw the next pitch, all long limbs and sharp corners. When had he gotten so big? More like a man than a boy, nearly as tall as his father already, and Garret was only twelve.

Jason found himself back in time, Garret a wobbly toddler, his wife Jeannie so young, with longer hair she used let fall around her shoulders. He could see himself on a podium at the town hall, the local news crew capturing footage of the picturesque family and the man who was running for town sheriff.

They'd been broke back then, he and Jeannie. She stopped teaching when Garret was born, unable to bear the thought of sending the baby to daycare. Jason wanted his wife to be able to stay home. He worked every overtime shift he could grab and tended bar at a friend's bar twice a week, while Jeannie looked after a coworker's son before and after school. Still, money was tight. They lived on hot dogs and rice mix, splurging only on a six-pack of beer to share Friday nights in front of the TV.

They were doing just that when a news teaser changed everything. "Local sheriff found dead of an apparent self-inflicted gunshot wound. Story at eleven."

"Holy...!" Jason turned wide eyes to his wife. "Bloom's dead?"

"He killed himself?"

"I just talked to him about the beat rotation schedule."

"Did something happen to him?"

"What do you mean?"

"I don't know." She uncurled her legs and walked to the refrigerator. "Divorce? Trouble at work?"

Jason ran his hand through his hair, grabbing a fistful of the dark curls. "Not that I know of."

"What's this going to mean for the department?"

He blew out air loudly. "Who knows."

"Who are the contenders for his job?"

"Gees, Jeannie, I don't know. The man just freakin' died."

"You could do it, Jason."

"Me?"

She nodded. "I've been thinking it for a while. You're popular on the force. You know what changes need to be made, changes that Bloom never seemed to get around to making."

He sank back on the couch. Him, be the sheriff? It would be more responsibility. He'd be able to see that the other officers' concerns were addressed. He'd make more money. Long before the eleven o'clock news aired, Jason had made up his mind. He would run for sheriff, and with Jeannie's help, he would win.

He couldn't have known Keith Patterson would run against him, a surname that he shared with the grocery store, the bank, and the biggest car dealership for a hundred miles. The Pattersons owned this town. They ran it. Jason may as well have been running against a Kennedy.

With every day that passed, Jason wanted the job more than the day before. Patterson had a bigger campaign, bolder, flashier, more expensive. Everywhere Jason turned he saw Keith Patterson's four-color signs mocking his own black and white ones, the other man's influence apparent at every turn. Jason's dream slipped further out of reach, and he began losing points in the polls.

You did what you had to do.

Sweat broke out along his neck.

It's a closed door.

At least he hoped it was closed. He imagined himself slamming a door in the face of a raging tiger, waiting for the cat's weight to hit the wood and see if it would hold.

Garret swung and missed, the third strike in a row. "This is freakin' stupid," said his son.

"Watch your mouth."

"Relax, Dad." He rolled his eyes. "I said 'freakin'', not 'fuckin'.'"

McDonald shook the ball in his fist at his son. "You will not speak that way to me. Do you understand? I won't have you using that sort of language."

"I was just saying freakin'!"

"That's unacceptable, and you know it." Jason's cell phone rang and he let it go.

"All the kids say it."

"You are not 'all the kids'."

"Oh right, I'm the son of the want-to-be-mayor."

Frustration mingled with anger and Jason fought to control his temper. The election was stressful enough without his son making it more difficult. He forced himself to take several deep breaths before allowing himself to speak. "Yes, I want to be mayor. We talked about this. Agreed, as a family, before I ever signed up to run." He took his glove off and stepped closer. "There's a spotlight on—"

"Spotlight on all of us, I know."

"That's right. It's not just me who's running for office."

Garret rolled his eyes. "It's the whole family."

"I know it's difficult for you." Jason's phone chirped, telling him he had a message. He checked it as they walked to the car.

The voice was familiar, adrenaline shooting into his belly. He had lost count of the nights he'd laid awake, fearing this moment. "Hi there, Jason. It's your old pal. Long time no see. I need you to do me another favor, Sheriff. Or should I call you Mayor McDonald?" The man chuckled. "I guess we'll see about that, won't we?"

Jason bent at the waist and threw up on his new sneakers. The neat world he had created for himself was about to come crashing down to the ground.

Chapter 8

Gwen sat upright in bed, her nose picking up the acrid scent of wood smoke. She flung the covers off her body and quickly got up, her pulse racing.

Twice before in her life she had awoken in such a fashion. The first time, she was eight years old and found her grandmother had fallen and broken her hip in the downstairs guest room. The second was when David was hurt in a car accident coming home from the airport.

For Gwen, smoke didn't always signal fire. But it signaled danger every time.

She flew down the darkened hallway toward Colin's room, clad in a simple satin sheath of vibrant pink. She opened his door and rushed to his beside, the light of the moon streaming in from an uncovered window. She touched the bare skin of his muscled arm, barely registering his nakedness.

"Colin, wake up."

He grunted in his sleep and moved to roll over.

She shook him. "Colin."

His eyes opened and he sat up. "What?"

"I had a dream, I smelled smoke. Something's wrong."

Colin inhaled deeply. "I don't smell anything."

"Trust me. Get up, you have to get up." She stood back and watched as his muscular form unfolded from the bed, clad only in a pair of black briefs. His body was beautiful, and she suddenly realized she should have gotten dressed. She crossed her arms over herself.

"What's wrong? There's no smoke..."

"I don't know. Go and check out the house. Quickly."

He rubbed his hands over his face, then grabbed a plaid bathrobe off a hook and headed downstairs, leaving the lights off and making his way through the moonlit house. He got two-thirds of the way down the stairs before he began to shout.

"Gwen! Get down here!" He turned and raced back to her, meeting her several steps down and grabbing her hand tightly as he reversed direction. "We have to get out of the house!"

Colin didn't stop running, pulling Gwen to match his steps, until he was more than a hundred feet from the building, finally releasing her hand and patting the pockets of his robe.

"What was that horrible smell?" asked Gwen.

"Propane. That's how the house is heated. Shit, my phone's inside." He put his hands on her upper arms. "Run to the neighbor's over there," he said, gesturing through a narrow band of trees. "Call 911. Tell them it's an emergency, that we have a propane leak." He took a step back toward the house.

"Where are you going?" she asked.

"I have to get my phone."

"No!" wailed Gwen, icy fear slicing through her consciousness.

"It will just take me a minute."

She was clutching at him now, digging in with her fingernails. "No you're not! I'm not going to lose you, too! Don't you go into that house, Colin Mitchell!"

He shrugged his shoulder, pulling his arm from her grasp. "Damn it, Gwen, go call 911."

"David! Stop this!"

Colin froze, his eyes staring into hers in the moonlit field. He ran his hands down her arms and spoke quietly. "I'm not David, Gwen."

Her mouth curled down and she stared at him, her chin quivering. "I know." She took a small breath. "Please don't go, Colin."

He lightly cupped her cheek. "Okay. We'll call 911 together."

She pulled him toward the tree line, and they began to jog, just as a fiery explosion lit the night sky. The force of the blast knocked them both to the ground.

~~~

Gwen walked into the Cigs-For-Less store in Beacon, New York wearing Colin's plaid bathrobe over her nightie. She held a hand to her temple, her eyes squinting against the light as she turned to the clerk.

He was young, with long brown hair stuck through the hole

in his brown baseball cap, and chuckled as he took in the sight of his latest customer.

Gwen's voice was a rasp. "Aspirin?"

He gestured to a small display of toiletries, watching as she grabbed a bottle of Advil and a six-pack of malt liquor, putting them both on the counter.

The clerk smiled, flashing a straight set of yellow teeth. "Rough night?"

She cast him a look steeped in camaraderie and trouble. "You have no idea. Pack of Marlboro reds, and I need to pick up a wire transfer."

He reached overhead for a form, which Gwen filled out. "I.D.?" he asked.

She blew out a puff of air and rolled her eyes. "With my clothes and a guy named Teeter, if you can believe that."

"That, I can," he said with a laugh. "You got a keyword for me?"

"Hudson."

He typed the information into a computer, then counted out a neat stack of bills from the register. "You feel better, now sweetheart. Go get yourself some shoes for them pretty feet." He winked.

Gwen winked back, holding up the beer. "I'll be feeling just fine in a minute."

She stepped outside and into the waiting cab.

Colin raised an eyebrow. "Make a new friend?"

"Colin, dear," she said, her eyes roving over his bare chest, "you're sitting in a taxi cab in your underpants. You are not in a position to criticize my new beau."

He snorted.

"Colt 45?" she offered. "It works every time."

He seemed to consider her offer, a grin pulling at one corner of his mouth. "Not right now."

Gwen leaned forward, passing the Marlboros to the cab driver. "Here you are, Samuel." He was skinny and olive-skinned, with thick dark hair and a lined face. In the short ride from Cold Spring, he had endeared himself to Gwen by offering her a blanket from the trunk of his taxi and carefully avoiding the obvious question of why these two people were barely clothed and in desperate need of transportation.

The memory of the explosion made Gwen shudder. The sound had been deafening, her own shock from the being thrown to the ground overwhelming. Colin hadn't missed a beat, hauling her to her feet and running urgent fingers over her arms and legs.

"Are you hurt? Anything broken?"

She shook her head. "Colin, your home!"

"We can't worry about that now. We need to get out of here."

Gwen hadn't understood. "Why?"

"This isn't an accident, Gwen."

Time seemed to stand still as she stared at him, the light of the fire casting an orange glow over his skin and all-too serious eyes. "What do you mean?" she whispered.

"Someone tried to kill us. Which means they're probably going to try again as soon as they realize they didn't succeed." He took her by the arm and began pulling her toward a different bank of trees. Gwen could hear sirens in the distance, and was suddenly aware of her bare feet on the dewy grass beneath her toes. Colin's words were beginning to hit home, adrenaline rushing through her. David had been killed, murdered on a ski slope, and now someone had tried to kill them as well.

She jogged alongside him as he sped up. "Where are we going?"

"The train station. Sometimes you can find a cab there late at night."

And so it was that they had found Samuel, leaning against the side of his yellow cab, smoking his last Marlboro Red.

He turned grateful eyes to her in the mirror as he smacked the new pack against his palm. "Thanks, ma'am. Do you mind…?"

Colin opened his mouth to object, but Gwen put her hand on his knee. "Of course not." She placated Colin with her eyes. "You're driving us all the way to Boston. You can smoke if you like. And please, call me Gwen." They'd been exceptionally lucky Samuel had agreed to take them on the long drive. They were paying him a king's ransom, money from the wire transfer

Rowan sent from Italy after they called him from Samuel's cell phone an hour ago. Yes, they'd been lucky to find Samuel indeed.

Gwen settled back against the seat, turning to Colin. "How long is the drive?"

"About three hours." He raised his voice. "There's a Wal-Mart up on Route 9, Samuel. I'd like you to go in and pick out some clothes for us to wear. Just jeans and t-shirts. And I'll need a cell phone of my own."

Samuel nodded. "Just tell me what size clothes."

Gwen watched the village pass by out her window, her eye drawn to a sign for The Dew Drop Inn. An image of Becky's cozy Craftsman appeared in her mind. The best friend of Gwen's niece Julie, Becky was dear to Gwen's heart, and the prospect of seeing her made her smile. *She always says I'm welcome anytime.*

She turned to Colin. "I know where we can stay in Boston."

Chapter 9

Becky flipped a purple pancake with a practiced flourish, the brightly colored batter spilling out the sides and onto the griddle with a pleasing hiss. A coffee maker gurgled behind her, its rich aroma mingling with the vanilla from the pancakes and making her moan out loud. "Damn that smells good," she said loudly.

"It really does," said Gwen from the doorway. "Pancakes?"

She nodded. "For you and your friend. I was dating this chef who taught me to make the most incredible pancakes."

Gwen's eyes widened. "Purple, I see."

Becky beamed. "That was my idea."

"Very nice touch. But I'm afraid Colin took the T to the city hours ago." Becky's house was just two blocks from the commuter train into downtown Boston.

Becky's face fell and she turned back to lift purple circles onto a plate. "Oh, when I didn't see him on the couch, I just figured he'd made his way upstairs during the night."

"We're not together."

A slow smile spread across Becky's face and she raised her eyebrows. "He looks at you like you're together."

"He does?"

"Hell, yeah."

"And how do I look at him?"

Becky nodded dramatically. "Like you got a little something for Christmas."

"Well," Gwen sighed, pouring herself a cup of coffee, "I'm afraid all I've received in that department is a big lump of coal."

"Have you been a good girl?"

"Of course."

"That's your problem." Becky brought the plate of pancakes to a large wooden table, along with a bottle of real maple syrup.

Gwen laughed. "It's good to see you, Becky."

Becky took a large bite of pancake, the purple fleshy insides showing between her teeth when she smiled. "You too."

"So tell me about the chef."

"What chef?"

"The one who gave you the pancake recipe."

"Oh," she said, waving her hand dismissively. "He wanted to play house."

"But you didn't."

Becky opened her arms, fingers splayed. "I already have a house."

"True."

"I just can't picture myself settling down with one man."

"Not ever?"

Becky grimaced, shaking her head. "It's not me, you know?"

Gwen nodded. "I do." She dragged a pancake through the thin river of syrup. "It's funny how we can see ourselves as singular, or as part of a duo. I've been single for eleven years, but I still catch myself thinking like a married woman."

"Do you still feel David..." she looked up to the ceiling, "...around?"

"I did. The first few years, especially. Sometimes he was so close, it was like he hadn't left at all. But gradually, it lessoned."

Becky took a sip of her coffee. It was dark and robust, with enough sugar and heavy cream to make it appeal to her childlike taste buds. "Do you still miss him?" she asked.

"I still wish things had turned out differently, but I suppose I've gotten used to living without him. It's been a long time." Gwen smiled softly. "Sometimes I feel like a very old woman."

Becky looked over Gwen's smooth, glowing skin, and took in the vibrant natural gold of her hair, her graceful posture, so like a dancer's. She said, "How old are you?"

"Thirty-six."

"No way."

Gwen nodded.

"My mom was forty-two when she had me."

"David and I wanted children."

"Do you still?"

Gwen shook her head. "Not by myself."

"Which brings us back to the beefcake you showed up with on my porch last night."

Gwen nearly spit out her food, and laughed. "I told you, there's nothing between Colin and me."

"Well, why the hell not? That man is hot. Smokin' hot, even."

"It's complicated."

Becky's eyes lit and she leaned forward. "Oh, I love complicated."

Gwen waved her away. "There's nothing, really."

"Spill it, Gwen." Becky stood, taking both their coffee cups to the counter for a refill. "I can be relentless. Want to see?" she asked, slamming the bright red mugs down too hard on the counter and flashing huge eyes just inches from Gwen's face.

Gwen sighed. "Oh, all right."

"Goody, goody!"

"Colin is the brother of David's best friend, Rowan."

"Okay."

"When David and I were dating, we went to a few parties at Rowan and Colin's house."

Becky flashed Gwen an excited smile as she covered her plate in syrup. "Go on."

"I found Colin attractive, of course, what woman wouldn't? But I wasn't interested in him that way."

"You were in love with David."

"Exactly. I was in love with David." She covered her face with her hand before taking a fortifying breath and continuing. "So one day, David and I were taking the train to another party at Rowan's house, and I was sort of dozing, but not really asleep. I was in that netherworld between the two."

Becky nodded. "Uh huh."

"And I was daydreaming about… Colin."

"Because he's hot. Smokin' hot. Hell, I was dreaming about him when I was cooking the pancakes."

"You have no idea," said Gwen, nodding. She took a slow sip of her coffee.

"And?" Becky asked.

"Oh, you won't believe it."

"You're killing me, Gwen."

A voice from the kitchen doorway turned both their heads

around. "She got to the party, all gorgeous with her hair wound up atop her head, this wispy little dress clinging to her in the summer's breeze."

Gwen turned back around, covering her mouth with her hand.

"And?" asked Becky.

"And I called her on it." He was standing shock still, his brown eyes molten and fixed on the back of Gwen's head.

"Called her on what?"

"The dream."

Becky's mouth dropped open and she gasped dramatically. "You called her on the dream?"

Colin crossed the threshold and stepped into the kitchen, never looking at Becky as he continued, "I could feel her. Every touch. Every thought that ran through her mind on that train. We shared something." He knelt before Gwen's chair, and she turned back around, her cheeks highly colored and vibrant as she stared at him.

"Holy shit," Becky said loudly.

"I never even got to touch her," he said, reaching out and lightly stroking Gwen's face, making her chin come up. "But I paid the price as if I had."

Becky leaned forward in her chair. "Price? What price?"

"I lost her."

"I was never yours to lose," Gwen said quietly.

"And I lost David," he said.

Becky's voice sounded like she was trying not to cry. "I thought David was Rowan's friend."

Gwen leaned back away from Colin and rose, breaking their connection. "David lived with Rowan and Colin from the time he was twelve."

"Oh my God, so he was like a brother to you!" cried Becky, her hand to her chest.

Colin stood, continuing to watch Gwen as she busied herself with the breakfast dishes. "Yes," he answered.

"What happened next?"

Colin's mouth formed a hard line. It was Gwen who spoke. "Colin got drunk and nearly made a pass at me. Rowan had to ask him to leave."

"Oh my God." Becky was shaking her head.

Colin looked at Becky for the first time. "Rowan did ask me to go, but I didn't give a shit what Rowan wanted. I left when David asked me to go."

Gwen quickly turned to face him, a dishtowel in her hand. "David asked you to leave? My David?"

He nodded.

Gwen turned back to the counter and made a brief show of trying to wipe it down before throwing the towel into the sink. She brushed past Colin on her way out of the kitchen. "Damn it, Colin."

Becky listened to Gwen's retreating footsteps as she took in the measure of the man across the room. He stared at the dishtowel, his hands in the pockets of his khakis. She liked him instantly. "It's not going to be easy," she said.

He shook his head. "No. No, it's not."

"But she's worth it," Becky said.

He nodded. "I know."

Satisfied with that answer, Becky set about finishing the dishes Gwen had abandoned. "How do you feel about purple pancakes?"

~~~

Colin's meeting with Randy Barr had gone well. A fellow deputy U.S. Marshal and an old friend of Colin's, Barr didn't ask questions when Colin asked him to print out the paperwork and meet him in Quincy early this morning.

But Barr didn't have access to Jerry's entire file. Those papers had been turned into ashes by the flames that ripped through Colin's house, and he had no way to get them again without going through Walker.

He rubbed at the tension in his shoulder. Colin was doubting his mentor, and that fact had his conscience and plain good sense doing backflips inside his brain. Walker was the person Colin trusted above all others, yet the man was one of only a handful who could have been responsible for the explosion.

He cursed under his breath. He'd spent the better part of two hours skimming documents from the trials that Jerry Ahearn testified in, getting up to speed on the major players involved in each of the three cases. That, combined with what Barr had been able to tell him about the modern day Irish Mafia in Boston, gave him a good idea of where to begin his search for information.

"There's a bar called Flynn's in Southie," Barr said. "It was the epicenter of the organization, back in its day. Now it's a local-hangout-turned-tourist-trap, decorated with newspaper stories of crimes and stuff. I've been there a couple times with my boss for lunch. They have a whole spread devoted to Jerry Ahearn."

"What, with coverage of the trial?"

Barr nodded. "Other stuff, too. Pictures, a gun. There's this big map that shows everything he testified about. It's really cool."

Maybe he'd find something at Flynn's that he was not finding in this stack of governmental paper. Colin frowned, dropping his pen and rubbing his temple. He reached for the plate Becky had brought him, selecting a tall turkey sandwich from the miniature buffet of lunch choices. There were three pigs in a blanket, two California rolls, and a small glass bowl of what smelled like peanut noodles with chopsticks sticking out.

Chewing distractedly, he glanced at the door and wondered when Gwen would return. She'd left the house after storming out the kitchen. Colin didn't understand why she was so angry, though he was beginning to get used to being confused around Gwen. What difference did it make if Rowan told him to leave the party, or it was David?

As if on cue, the door opened and Gwen entered the room with Becky's little Pug on a leash. Lucy was dancing happily at Gwen's feet while she tried to unsnap the collar. "Oh, what a good girl. Did you enjoy your walk?"

Colin stared at Gwen, his pulse racing in anticipation of their exchange. *I could spend the rest of my life looking at this woman, even if she is mad as all hell.*

She met his eyes. "I'm sorry, Colin," she said, with a tone that implied she was not sorry at all.

"Thank you. Why were you so angry?"

She crossed her arms over her chest. "I loved David very

much."

"Gwen, did I ever imply otherwise?"

"If he asked you to leave, then he was aware of your intentions."

Colin took a sip of his water, deliberately weighing his words. "They weren't just my intentions, Gwen." Her eyes darkened and realization dawned on Colin. "That's it, isn't it? You're upset because David knew there was something between us."

"There was nothing…"

He raised a hand to stop her protest. "But that's it, right? You're upset because David knew."

"Yes."

She looked like she was about to cry, and Colin felt a momentary concern. "You didn't do anything wrong, Gwen. You never cheated on your husband."

She shrugged. "I know. But if he asked you to leave…"

"I get it." Colin watched her win the fight for composure, gently rubbing her eye with her knuckle. Even under duress, she was lovely. How many years had he been missing this woman? Wishing for one more chance to find a way into her life?

No, not just into her life. I want it all. Everything.

His mouth had gone dry, and he felt his eyes glued to her face, waiting for her to glance his way like a dog waiting for a morsel to drop from the table above. When she did finally raise her lashes and meet his stare, she smiled prettily.

The words were out before he could think better of them. "Someday, Gwen, we're going to be together."

He watched as the remark affected her, eyes dilating and a soft pink glow moving into her cheeks. Her rounded bottom lip hung separate from its partner, teasing him with its invitation, even as her words belied her face. "No, Colin."

"Not now. I know you're not ready. But when you are, I'll be here."

Her gaze dropped to the paperwork on the table. "What are you doing?" she asked.

"Going through the papers Barr gave me."

"Were you able to get copies of everything you lost in the

fire?"

"Not even close. These are just the transcripts from the trials Jerry testified in."

"What have you learned?"

"I found this." He opened a binder.

She shook her head. "What am I looking at?"

"A document from discovery. It wasn't used in the trial, but just got stuck in the file with everything else, looks like. It gives an address for Jerry Ahearn's aunt Bernice. Apparently, he was living with her for a time before he turned himself in to the feds."

"I don't understand what this means."

"I'm just thinking, if Jerry felt safe enough to hide out there all those years ago, maybe he felt safe enough to return there. Especially if Walker was right and Jerry's back in the fold."

"What did your contact at the Marshal's office have to say?"

"He hasn't heard anything definitive, but he thinks it's possible. Jerry's testimony put away two of the top three guys, then the third one died a year later of natural causes. There's been a lot of upheaval. Nearly everyone he betrayed is no longer with the company, so to speak."

"But still, you think they'd trust him after he testified against their own people?"

Colin tilted his head to the side. "You have to remember, even within the organization there's a struggle for power. Jerry turned against some people, but not all. According to Deputy Barr, Jerry may have played his hand strategically. Everyone he testified against was old blood. He actually helped the new boss take over."

Gwen leaned forward and rested her chin on her hand. "You mean, he might even be considered a faithful servant to the organization."

"Maybe, yes."

"When are we going to the aunt's house?"

"What you mean 'we', Kemo Sabe?"

She dropped her chin and looked at him through her lashes. "I'm coming with you, Colin."

He began gathering the papers back into a neat pile. "No."

Gwen stood, pushing her chair into the table with

uncharacteristic force. "Yes."

A reply was quick to his tongue, but Colin met her fiery eyes and paused. She was the one who came to him, suspecting David's death was not an accident. She was the one whose quick thinking and acting had gotten them this far. Besides, he would call less attention to himself at the bar if he wasn't alone. "I want to stop at a bar my contact told me about first. And you can come, Gwen, but promise me this. If I believe it's too dangerous for you to do something, you'll listen to me and step back."

"Deal. Where are we going?"

"Flynn's. A bar in Southie."

"Fabulous." She checked her watch. "I could use a pint to wash down those purple pancakes, couldn't you?"

Chapter 10

Gwen felt Colin's hand on the small of her back, guiding her around a large buckle in the sidewalk. They parked Becky's car several blocks away, the nearest spot they could find in the tightly woven neighborhood of houses that existed solely with on-street parking. There were no front lawns here, with houses butting up against the sidewalk like storefronts on an old fashioned Main Street.

Gwen felt as though she was tromping directly through the family rooms of these people. She heard snippets of conversation, bits of television shows and the smell of something baking. "I wonder what it would be like to live here," she said.

"Crowded."

She clucked her tongue. "I think it's lovely. Quaint, with a modern vibe."

He looked around at the few people on the street. "We're at least ten years older than most of the people living here."

"Ah, but I am young at heart." She winked at him. "You would stand out like a sore thumb."

He glared at her, one side of his mouth hitched up into a grin.

She worked to keep pace with his long strides, the click of her high-heeled sandals tapping on the concrete. Walking next to him like this, she could almost believe no time had passed, that they were teenagers again with the world at their feet and the future at their door, as if David and Rowan were just a step behind.

Instead of a lifetime away.

Gwen found herself mentally searching the air for her husband's spirit, so longingly did she miss him in that moment. But there was no trace of him in her mind, only a memory that had grown tired of being remembered, and she sighed aloud.

Colin turned his head at the sound, opening his palm to her as they walked, and she placed her hand in his. It felt warm and solid, a strong hand to go with the strong man at her side.

They turned a corner, the change in direction blowing the scent of him right into her face. Was that cologne, or just the smell of him alone? It was both familiar and unnerving to smell a man so intimately.

"Are we almost there?" she asked.

"On the next corner."

The area was splattered with more businesses, storefronts clamoring for their attention. Chinese food. A diner. A dry cleaning shop. Up ahead she could see a neon orange sign that read "Flynn's" shining in the midday summer sun, and felt her stomach twirl with anxiety. She turned to Colin and found him watching her.

"Just follow my lead," he said, seeming to understand her reservation. They reached the bar and he pulled open the wooden door, holding it for her to enter first.

Gwen stopped short. "Do you want to sit at the bar?" she asked.

"Yes."

There were three people sitting there already, each seemingly alone, and Gwen smiled graciously at each one as she passed. "Hi, there. Hello. How are you?" she asked, finally reaching two black barstools at the end of the bar and sitting gracefully on one.

The bartender put coasters down in front of them. "What can I get for you?" he asked, raising an eyebrow.

"I'd like a black Russian, please," said Gwen.

"And I'll take a Glenlivet on the rocks."

"I was thinking about a nice Scotch too, but the black Russian seemed more cloak and dagger."

"Vodka martini. Now that's cloak and dagger."

"Bond," she said in a deep voice.

"James Bond," he finished. "I thought you wanted a pint?"

"Beer before liquor, never sicker."

"Oh. Well, now it all makes sense." Colin turned to the bartender. "So, this used to be a hangout for the Irish Mafia?"

"Sure was. This place controlled more of Boston than City Hall in the 70s."

Gwen turned to take in the room. Its walls were covered in

photographs and framed newspaper stories. A small spotlight illuminated a handgun in an acrylic box. An enormous map took up the entire wall opposite the bar.

"Oh my goodness, is that a painting?" asked Gwen, rising to her feet.

"Sure is. The whole city of Boston."

She crossed to the map, climbing into a booth to get a closer view. The mural was large enough in scale to depict individual streets in the city, many labeled by name. But it was the detail that took her breath away. "Colin, come look at this!" she said.

He slid across the opposite seat. "Holy cow."

Drawn on the map were what seemed like hundreds of images—a truck overturned, a building on fire—along with descriptions of events in the history of the mafia. From notorious crimes to the men responsible for their commission, it was all detailed here in fine painting and the tiniest of brushstrokes.

Gwen's arm shot up to point. "Michael "The Boxer" Gallente kills Town Councilman Berger!"

"Gwen, look at this one." Colin pointed to a painted cameo next to a textbox in the middle of the ocean. "It's Jerry."

She scrambled out of the booth and moved to the next table over, reading, "Jerry Ahearn, trusted brother, cast out to sea after testifying against members of the organization." Her eyes rested on the image of the man, so like her David. The resemblance sent a shiver to her core. "Oh, my goodness."

"This is crazy," said Colin. "It's all here. Everything from the court documents."

"And a lot more, I'd say," said Gwen, sitting back on her haunches. Her eyes took in the enormity of the map as she sipped at her smooth drink.

Meet the in-laws.

The moment was surreal. David Beaumont was a good, decent man, but he was connected to this horror by blood and experience. It may have even killed him. The thought had cold awareness flooding her center. One of these people may have killed my husband.

Her eyes returned to the portrait of Jerry Ahearn. David's father. She felt in her heart that they would find him, that this

man's introduction was in her future. Gwen realized with some
surprise that her drink was empty. "I'm going to get another
drink. Would you like one?"

Colin looked up from his examination of the map. "I'll get it
for you."

She waved him off. "Not a problem. You go ahead." She
gestured to the mural and went back to the bar, ordering herself a
pint of Guinness.

A voice in her ear made her jump. "Gwen!" She turned and
looked down the bar to see who called her. Three seats down, on
an empty barstool, she imagined she could see her late husband.
He raised his own pint glass to her and sipped, then pointed
wildly over the head of an old man sitting next to him.

Gwen looked to Colin, who was still absorbed in the map,
then turned back to David.

He was gone.

Her eyes narrowed. It certainly wasn't the first time she had
imagined her husband's ghost, but it was the first time he had
tried to communicate something to her. She observed the old
man as he worked the coaster under his drink in a circle,
spinning it absentmindedly as he watched the news on a muted
television screen.

Gwen always enjoyed meeting someone new, and she saw
no reason this introduction should be any different. She scooted
onto the seat David had occupied and offered the man a big
smile. "I'm Gwen," she said warmly, extending her hand.

"Martin." His eyes were watery and blue, their depths
clearly expressing his joy at being joined by a beautiful woman.
His fine white hair was neatly combed, his jacket identifying him
as a member of the local freemason's union.

"You're a mason," she said, impressed. "I have a great
appreciation for artistry. Walls and stone walkways, strong brick
buildings and stately concrete constructions."

He smiled, revealing neatly polished teeth. "I been a mason
for forty-two years." He gestured out the front door of the bar. "I
laid the foundation for the Waller Building with my bare hands
and a trowel."

"How interesting!" she said, picking up her pint and sipping the strong brew freely. "There is a barn on my property with a cobblestone foundation. The barn itself has been rebuilt twice that I know of, but that foundation's still going strong. They don't build them like they used to."

"Where's your property?"

She smiled generously. "In Vermont, about half an hour outside of Barre."

"You didn't sound like you was from around here."

She shook her head. "No, I'm not. But it's a beautiful town. I might stay a while."

"Your friend from Vermont, too?"

Gwen raised her eyebrows. No, he's from Cold Spring. Just north of New York City."

His eyes widened. "Cold Spring?"

She nodded. "Yes."

"Now, ain't that a coincidence."

"What?"

"I just ran into an old buddy of mine the other day, used to live in Cold Spring. I hadn't seen him in years."

"Oh, no?"

Martin shook his head. "He got himself in some trouble a while back. Did some time."

She turned completely and faced Martin, wondering if this kind-hearted old man had information that could help her. "I'm looking for my father-in-law. His name is Jerry. Do you know him, Martin?"

~~~

Graham Walker was double-parked, the corner of his Grand Marquis closer to the bumper of a Jeep Cherokee than most people could manage without swapping paint. He wore dress slacks and a button-down shirt, having long ago ceased to be comfortable in clothes of a more casual nature.

Walker had been sitting behind a desk for more years than he cared to count, and believed on any given day he was able to accomplish more there than he could out in the field. He was an administrator, through and through. He followed the rules. He documented everything. But he knew as he sat in his car outside of Flynn's that today's events would never be written down and filed away by him or anyone else.

This one was personal.

Through the window of the bar, he could see Colin Mitchell looking at something on the wall, and Walker wondered if the widow had accompanied Colin to Boston. It would be easier if she had. He put his palm over his mouth and pressed in his cheeks.

Hell, it would be easier if Mitchell hadn't come at all.

A car honked its horn as it worked to maneuver around the Marquis. Walker twirled his wedding band on his hand, forcing it over the knuckle and back again, oblivious to the other driver's difficulty. He wanted a cigarette, despite having given them up eighteen years earlier, and he desperately wanted a drink.

The man's house blows up in the middle of the night, and he doesn't even call me.

Colin Mitchell was like a son to Walker. He even looked like Walker's son, when the boy had been alive. Tom Walker had been killed in a motorcycle accident when he was twenty-three, leaving his father to his job with the U.S. Marshal's Office and his mother to lose her mind. June had never been able to recover from Tommy's death, slowly slipping away to depression and alcoholism until she required constant care.

Mentoring Colin had filled a need in Walker's spirit that had gone unmet since Tommy passed away. Walker was meant to be a teacher, an instructor. A leader of leaders. Colin was meant to be the next in command, a designation that Walker conferred as much as recognized.

He cut himself loose like a kite in the wind.

What did it mean, that Colin hadn't called his trusted boss when someone tried to kill him as he slept in his bed?

He had no idea where to find Colin until Deputy Barr accessed the records on the Ahearn trials this morning. Walker had put that case to bed himself, tramped the dirt down overtop when Ahearn got out of prison. He sure as hell didn't want anyone digging around in that graveyard without his permission.

That's what burned him. Colin had permission.

He could have asked for the records again himself, and Walker would have given them. But Colin hadn't done that.

Instead, he ran off to Boston and had Barr pull the transcripts. There could be only one reason for that, and the reality was chafing at Walker's collar.

He thinks I had something to do with it.

His thick fingers worked to twist his ring, popping it over the knuckle. A rap on his window had Walker turning his head. A uniformed police officer gestured for him to put the window down.

"You can't park here, sir. Move along."

Walker hesitated, the badge in his pocket heavy on his mind, his desire for anonymity winning out over expediency.

"Sorry, officer," he said, putting the car into drive and flashing a harmless grin. He drove once around the block and returned to the bar, finding both the police officer—and Colin Mitchell—gone.

Chapter 11

"Martin said he talked to Jerry for about fifteen minutes, but he has no idea how to find him," said Gwen.

Colin drove up the onramp to 93 South. "Did you believe him?"

"Not at all. I don't even think he wanted me to believe him."

"What do you mean?"

Gwen put her hand on the dashboard of the car, her heart suddenly pounding in her chest. "I don't want to go this way."

"But this is the way to Becky's."

"We'll have to find another way. Get off at the next exit, please." Her voice held an element of alarm.

"What's the matter, Gwen?"

"I don't know. I just know that as soon as you started driving on this road, I felt we were in danger. We need to get off of it, now."

Colin shook his head as he quickly moved to the right-hand lane. "You get feelings like this a lot?"

"Often enough that I know when to listen."

"Do you know what kind of…" he stopped speaking mid-sentence, his eyes wide on the rear-view mirror.

"What's wrong?"

"I think we're being followed." Gwen immediately moved to turn around, and Colin put his hand on her knee. "Don't look now."

"What do you see?"

"A big sedan. It got on with us, then cut over when I did and got off, too." He put on his turn signal and pulled into the parking lot of a convenience store. "What are you going to do now, mister?" he asked the other car. It continued past the entrance without slowing down. Colin pulled back onto the road, headed back toward the expressway.

"North please, not south," said Gwen.

"I want you to turn around in your seat and look out for that car."

They were at the very top of the on-ramp before she spoke. "I see it. They're just getting on the on-ramp."

"Damn it."

"Coming our way, quickly."

Colin pressed hard on the accelerator and slipped into the passing lane. The late afternoon traffic was oddly light, providing little cover.

Gwen had spent time in Boston before she and David were married, teaching art classes while he composed his first soundtrack. Her brain worked to remember the exits ahead. "Up over that hill, there's an exit with a rotary. A bunch of roads meet. If we can get there first, he won't know which way we went."

"Good idea."

Gwen watched as the needle on the speedometer crossed one hundred and continued to rise. She closed her eyes, saying a silent prayer for their own safe travels and those of the drivers around them on the road. A feeling of peace was punctuated by clear direction. "Take the first right on the rotary," she said to Colin.

"Where does it go?"

"I have no idea. Just take it."

"What the lady wants," he said under his breath as the car crested the hill. The exit ramp was visible five hundred feet down the road, and he hit the breaks quickly to take the turn. "Can he see us?"

"Not yet, not yet..." she said, watching the top of the hill behind them. They were nearly out of view when the other car popped over the horizon. "Yes!"

"Is he following?"

"Yes."

A sharp turn in the road forced Gwen against the car door.

"Sorry," said Colin.

"Quite all right."

The exit ramp circled down a full level beneath the highway, shielding the other car from view. Colin took the first right on the rotary at a speed that made her cringe. Gwen squinted through the trees, trying to make out the other vehicle. "He didn't see us," she said, the relief in her voice evident.

"Clearly, we got someone's attention at that bar."

"Not a good someone, either. I wonder if it was Martin," said Gwen.

"You said you didn't believe him."

She squinted her eyes. "Well, no. Not completely. He was endearing, but I just got the feeling he wasn't being completely truthful with me. Then he got talking about the riptide up at Sandwich Beach this time of year."

"Sandwich?"

"Yes. He said it's on the Cape."

"I know where it is." Colin shifted in his seat and sat up straighter. "Do you think he was trying to give you a clue?"

"I'm not sure. Maybe."

"That map was interesting, too."

"What did you find out?"

"It was like a complete history of the Irish Mafia in Boston, with key events, accomplishments, deaths and arrests. It even had information on politicians they controlled, and how many girlfriends they had. It was nuts."

"Was there anything else about Jerry?"

Colin nodded. "His face was painted on a pigeon's body next to Mickey Brady, the former leader who was brought down by Jerry's testimony, and on a rat's body next to Brady's right-hand man."

"People he testified against?"

"Yes. But he wasn't even mentioned next to two others, who he also testified against."

"That is strange."

"Our buddy, Mike Gallente, had his own entry. It said he was a beloved member of the organization who was tragically incarcerated."

"That would support the theory that Jerry helped to bring in a new regime."

"I thought of that myself. I think tomorrow we should go to the aunt's house and look for Jerry."

"Agreed. Perhaps we should check out Sandwich as well. We'll just find a hotel for the night, and I'll let Becky know we're not heading back to her place."

"At all?"

Gwen sighed. "I feel like we would be bringing danger to her door. I don't want to do that."

"Agreed. I'm going to give Rowan a call and have him wire us more money. Let's put some distance between us and our friend, then we'll find a hotel for the night."

"Sounds like a plan," he said confidently, but he couldn't help but wonder who was chasing after them, and when they would meet again.

~~~

Colin hung up the phone and placed it on the hotel room desk. Rowan was sending more money. Colin rubbed his face. The fact that he had only the shirt on his back and a prepaid cell was upsetting to Colin, who never left home without his wallet and smartphone.

He and Gwen had stopped to buy more clothes when they passed a department store, using all but a hundred dollars of their cash-on-hand. They didn't have the money for a second hotel room, even if one had been available.

He heard the water come on and knew Gwen had gotten into the shower. The image of her naked body so near to him would normally have gotten his pulse racing, but as he sank onto the bed he was overwhelmed with guilt and self-loathing.

It was all his fault.

An image of David formed in his mind, as much as a brother as Rowan ever was. Their estrangement had been hell for Colin, even worse now that he was able to admit his responsibility. At the time, he insisted to himself that Gwen was as guilty as he, truly believing she had feelings for him instead of David. Now he knew he'd been wrong. Gwen may have been attracted to him, but she only ever loved her husband. Colin had been a young pompous ass who cared more about himself than he cared about his own family.

He had seen only what he wanted to believe, and it had cost him his relationship with David and hurt the woman he claimed to care for.

What would it have been like, to have been friends with

them both? Visits to Vermont, skiing with his friend. Maybe he even would have been on the mountain next to David when his past came back to haunt him.

An image played in his mind like a movie, himself skiing off the lift beside David, at his side when he first recognized Michael and knew there might be trouble. He felt a physical pain in his abdomen at the possibilities lost, an opportunity to save the man he so cared for.

The past was in the past. There was nothing he could do to change it, but he could damn sure respect the memory of his friend and stay away from his wife—a woman who clearly still didn't want a relationship with Colin.

It was the least he could do. He would fix the mistakes in his past, make amends as best he could. He would find the person responsible for David's death, make them pay. And he would send Gwen on her way, free to make a new life with someone else. She was young, beautiful. She could marry again, become a mother if she wanted. Colin pictured her cradling a sleeping infant with rosy cheeks, a physical pain appearing in his gut at the knowledge that the baby would never be his.

Colin moved to the bed away from the window, leaving the one with a view for Gwen. He wouldn't bother her tonight, or ever again. Colin had to find a way to get her to safety and look for Jerry on his own. Now that he was seeing clearly, he understood that he had only allowed her to join him on this trip because he wanted the chance to be physically close to her, a mistake that could have gotten her killed.

I am an arrogant ass.

The water turned off and Colin braced himself for the evening ahead. Suddenly nervous, he didn't know what to do with Gwen if he wasn't actively pursuing her. He busied himself with the television, mindlessly flipping through channels as he waited for Gwen to come out of the bathroom.

~~~

Gwen ripped the tags off the pink brassiere and held it up to the light, its fine lace and shimmering ribbons mocking her serious expression. She had already slipped on the matching panties and stood in the steamy bathroom as she finally admitted the truth.

She wanted Colin. She wanted Colin very much.

The lingerie set had caught her eye in the department store and she thought nothing of it, tucking the items under a dress and two shirts already in her hands. But more than an hour later as she dressed to confront Colin in the intimacy of the hotel room, she knew she had purchased the items in anticipation of something more.

Gwen closed her eyes and hugged the bra to her chest, both for fear of crossing the line she long ago drew in the sand and for her own eagerness to be done with pretenses. She and Colin had driven in silence after they lost their pursuer, a comfortable silence that reminded Gwen of everything she had once held in her hand and had long since learned to do without.

Friendship. Companionship. Physical love.

She loved the feel of him beside her in the car, the strength of his spirit and the scent of his skin. They drove along the country roads and Gwen knew she would make love to this man, to give in to the energy that connected them like electricity. It was not a fantasy this time, but a plan.

An overdue plan to give in to desire.

There would be no going back, though she would be the first to admit there were bound to be regrets. Gwen finished dressing by slipping a wide-necked jersey dress over her bra and panties, not knowing what tomorrow would bring for her and Colin, but knowing exactly what she wanted from today. She stepped into the hotel room as the last rays of the setting sun fell across the room.

Colin sat on one of the beds, legs stretched out before him, arms crossed behind his head as he watched her. The pose would have made her nervous just hours before, but now she welcomed the dance in her stomach. Gwen had never given half her love, and she was not about to start this evening.

"Good shower?" he asked.

"Mmm hmm. Your turn." Her eyes went to the TV.

"I'm not watching this. Go ahead and change it," he said as he stood.

"I don't want to watch TV," she said, her eyes telling him

what she wanted instead.

The energy hummed between them. He stared at her for several seconds before looking away, then stood and walked into the bathroom.

Gwen squinted against the orange rays of the sun and crossed her arms over her chest, feeling goose bumps along her arms as she did.

Be happy, Gwen.

The words were clear in her mind, though they were not spoken aloud. David's spirit was light, but undoubtedly present.

"Thank you," she whispered, a smile touching her lips as she closed her eyes and lingered in the moment. When she opened them, the sun had slipped beneath the horizon, coating the room in a softened dusk. The rush of water told her Colin had turned on the shower.

Be happy.

The cell phone rang and Gwen reached to answer it. "Hello?"

"Gwen, it's Rowan. How are you holding up?"

A flash of guilt went through her at the reminder of the hunt for David's killer, but she allowed it to recede as quickly as it had come. "Pretty well, all things considered."

"I'm flying into Logan. I just boarded the plane."

"You don't have to—"

"Sure I do, Gwen."

She considered for a moment how she would feel if she was an ocean away from these events, and understood that Rowan needed to join them. "Yes, of course you do. I'm sorry. When does your flight get in?" She wrote the information down and tucked the paper in her purse.

"Let me talk to Colin."

"He's in the shower."

There was a pause on the line. "All right. I'll see you in the morning. I don't know if my cell will work in the states or not."

"We'll be waiting for you, Rowan. Have a good flight."

A tension settled between Gwen's shoulder blades at the memory of Rowan's role all those years ago. She suspected her husband's best friend would not approve of her and Colin being together, and mentally decided to wait until morning to tell Colin that Rowan was on his way. She didn't want anything to come between her and Colin this evening—not David's memory or Rowan's hostility.

~~~

Colin dressed in the steamy bathroom, his damp skin sticking to the fresh cotton of his new t-shirt. It aggravated him as it pulled at him, the action seeming more difficult for the situation that awaited him outside the door.

He needed to apologize to her.

He needed to get her the hell out of harm's way.

He needed a football field between them and a cold shower.

He cursed under his breath as he tugged a pair of crisp blue jeans over his thighs. She wasn't going to go willingly, that much was for sure. Colin considered whether to discuss it with her at all, or simply tell her what was going to happen as he headed to Becky's house to drop her off.

He brushed his teeth and ran his fingers through his short hair before he opened the door, and his heart stopped beating. Gwen reclined against the pillows, wearing a sexy smile and a thoughtful look.

"Hi," she said softly.

Colin felt his blood stir and tramped down his desire. *Haven't you done enough to this woman? Do you need to keep pestering her for the smallest affection?*

"Hey." He turned to the desk and began digging through it. "You hungry?"

"I am. What do you have in mind?"

He could think of a few things, but none of them were on a menu. "I don't care. Pizza. Subs. Whatever you want."

Gwen walked to stand next to him, looking at the selection over his shoulder. She smelled like sweet soaps and something flowery, and she was standing too close. Reaching over him, she pointed. "Do you like Thai?"

"What, like seaweed and stuff?"

She chuckled and lightly hit his shoulder. "No. It's simple food, usually spicy. It has a light, balanced finish."

"Sounds like seaweed."

Gwen picked up the menu and began looking. "I want this. You can have pizza."

Colin could still feel his skin tingling where she had touched him. "I'll try it. Just order me something that's not too scary." He watched as she picked up the cell phone and dialed, tossing her golden curls before putting the phone to her ear.

"About forty-five minutes," she said, coming to sit beside him. Gwen's hip was next to his on the bed, nearly touching, driving him crazy. He turned to her, his gaze questioning. Was it his imagination or was she flirting with him?

It would be so easy to kiss her. Just like that. Bend his head and do what he always wanted to do around her. Instead, he heard himself say the words that needed to be said. "I'm sorry, Gwen."

Her brows drew together. "What for?"

He stood and began to pace. "So many things. I don't even know where to start." How did you explain to someone that you held yourself responsible for everything that had ever gone wrong in her entire life?

"I'm listening."

"The party. When I made a pass at you, embarrassed you. I shouldn't have done that."

He watched her face soften, her full bottom lip curling up on one side. "Thank you."

"I hurt David, too." He shook his head. "He was as important to me as my own brother, and I didn't give a damn how he was feeling. I tried to steal the woman he loved. I would have done it in a heartbeat if you let me." He took a deep breath. "Now he's gone, and I can't ever fix that. Apologize. Make it right."

Gwen stood and took a step toward him. "He knows, Colin."

"Bullshit," he said under his breath.

She came closer, resting her hand on his shoulder. "He does."

Their eyes locked, absolution passing between them like consent. Colin slowly nodded. She seemed so sure of herself, he could almost believe it. "I hope you're right." He saw her stare drop to his own lips, an answering fire igniting in his belly.

Hadn't he just apologized for this very thing? Not a minute later, he was already imagining kissing her. He took a step back and turned away. He had to make her understand everything. Once she did, she would never look at him like that again.

"David and I used to go skiing together all the time," he said.

"I know."

He spoke past the knot in his throat that worked to stop all communication. "Maybe I would have been there."

He heard her approach before she grabbed his shoulder and turned him around to face her. She looked angry. "Stop this, Colin. It is not your fault David died." Color flooded her cheeks as she shook her finger at him. "You are not the one who killed him, you are not responsible for his death. Do you understand me?"

"I should have been there. I should have been in his life. Who knows? I could have made a difference…"

Gwen stepped on her tiptoes and pressed her mouth to his, stopping the flow of words and shocking him into silence. She pulled back and met his surprised eyes. "He loved you, Colin, and he missed you, just as I did."

"You missed me?"

She nodded her head, wide-eyed. "But I was too ashamed to encourage David to contact you."

"Ashamed?" He held on to her when she would have stepped back.

"The attraction between you and me was never one-sided, Colin. With you gone, I didn't have to feel uncomfortable. I knew David missed you, and I just let it go because it was easier that way." She wiped at a tear that had fallen onto her cheek. "What kind of person does that make me? I never cheated on my husband, but I cheated him out of the family he loved."

Colin watched a second tear fall from her lashes, and bent his head to kiss it away. Every reason he had devised for keeping Gwen at arm's length vanished in that instant. She was here, of her own free will. She knew everything that haunted him and she forgave him.

She reached up and pulled him tighter to her, finding his lips with her own. Colin's heart swelled, knowing that she wanted him, that she cared for him, that she'd missed him. What had always been a physical attraction turned into something so much more, deeper, more meaningful. Colin was lost in her, lost in the moment, lost in their loving. Evening turned to nighttime and kisses to sweet passion, inching closer to the morning's light and what Colin knew he must do.

Protect this woman, as he had failed to protect her husband. He only hoped she would be able to forgive him when she awoke in the morning to find him gone.

Chapter 12

Dear Gwen,

I love you. Last night meant everything to me.

But I can't protect you if you're with me, and I can't bear the thought of anything happening to you. I called Becky—she's coming to pick you up. Don't go back to her house, just in case. Find somewhere safe. I'll see you as soon as I can.

Colin

~~~

Gwen let the paper fall from her hand and sat on the edge of the bed. She had awoken slowly, languid memories of her night with Colin stretching through her mind. Her fantasies hadn't done the man justice. When she wanted him again, she reached out for him with a cat-like purr, only to find his side of the bed cold and empty.

"Colin?" she called, sitting up. Her body felt funny, not used to lovemaking, and it made her feel good and alive.

She walked to the window and pulled back the curtain, light streaming in from the bright summer's day, making her flinch. It was then that she saw the note on the table.

Anger was slow to percolate, gradually taking over where shock had settled first. She was hurt, betrayed. Had he known that he would leave her, even as he became her lover? She had opened her heart and shown him the love that was growing inside, believing he was doing the same. But he was preparing to deceive her, to summarily lift her out of a situation that was vital to her wellbeing and drop her onto the sidelines like a spectator.

How dare he?

Gwen stood, just as a knock came at the door. She reached for a towel and covered herself before opening it. One look at Becky's sheepish expression told her all she needed to know. "Good morning, dear," said Gwen. "Just so you know, we are going after that damnable man, no matter what he wants. Are you on the side of righteousness?"

Becky's eyes lit. "Abso-freakin-lutely."

"Wonderful. Make yourself at home while I get dressed."

The house was small and gray, its weathered shingles somewhat neglected. A cool breeze came in off the ocean, making a porch swing rock on its own and momentarily startling Colin. He walked up the wooden steps, which creaked beneath his feet, and rapped soundly on the door.

He could feel his sidearm in its holster, the weight of it adding both security and concern, his senses already on high-alert from knocking on what he believed was Jerry Ahearn's front door. Lace curtains moved to the side, revealing a boy with curling brown hair. "Can I help you?" he asked as he opened the door.

"I'm looking for someone."

The boy raised his eyebrows.

"An old friend. He used to live here." Colin's heart hammered in his chest. "His name's Jerry. Do you know him?"

The boy rolled his eyes. "Um, yeah. He's my dad. But he's not home."

Jerry was his father?

Colin's eyes searched his features for any similarity to David. Their coloring was completely different, the boy's warm skin tone suggesting his background was not completely Irish as David's had been.

David's brother.

Half-brother, he corrected. Adele died when David was six; this boy must have been born much later.

"How old are you?" asked Colin.

He eyed him wearily. "Who are you?"

He froze, unsure of what to say, just as a voice called from the door behind them. "Luke, who is at the door?" An attractive brunette appeared, wiping her hands on a towel. Her eyes met Colin's and recognition slammed into his consciousness, making him reel.

The woman's hands jerked and she dropped the towel, covering her mouth.

"Emma?" Colin gasped, his voice too loud as he stepped toward her, the boy all but forgotten. This wasn't really happening. It simply wasn't possible. He had looked for her for nearly a year, exhausted every possible avenue to find her.

The boy looked from Colin to the woman and back. "Mom, what's going on?"

"Mom?" said Colin, his eyes raking over the boy's face a second time, urgent now, easily noting her similarity to the brunette. "Oh, sweet Jesus…" He raised a shaking hand to the boy's cheek and he pulled away from him, just as his mother reached out and hauled the boy to her side.

Emma's voice shook when she spoke. "I can explain everything, Colin."

~~~

Rowan Mitchell stepped out of the terminal and into the bright sunshine of a New England summer's day. It had been too damn long since he set foot on American soil, the glamour of being an expat in Italy having long ago lost its appeal. He hadn't even seen his brother since his own wedding to Tamra three years earlier, an unconscious grimace crossing his face at the thought of his wife.

"Rowan!" Gwen was walking toward him in the sunshine, a bright smile lighting her face.

He held out his arms to her. "It's been too long," said Rowan. "You look fantastic."

"Thank you," she said, reaching up to pinch his cheeks. "And congratulations! I hear you are married. And a father! How wonderful."

He bobbed his head as words failed him, his recent wounds too fresh and overwhelming for conversation. "A lot has changed."

"She must be something, to have stolen your heart and taken you away to a foreign land," Gwen said with a wink.

Oh, she's something, all right. They began walking away from the terminal. "Where's Colin?"

Rowan had been waiting to get his hands on his younger brother since he realized Colin and Gwen were sharing a room at the hotel. *He's in the shower,* Gwen had said.

The thought had driven Rowan half crazy all the way across the Atlantic, imagining Colin doing all manner of inappropriate things to cajole the innocent widow into his bed. Why couldn't his damnable brother leave Gwen well enough alone? Why did he always have to push it, try for a relationship that was never meant to be? The thought that Colin would pursue Gwen now, with David dead, made Rowan extremely angry. It was like spitting on his best friend's grave.

"I'm not sure where Colin is. He was gone when I awoke this morning."

Rowan didn't miss the intimate phrasing, but decided to bite his tongue. More concerning right now was the fact that his brother had abandoned her. "He just left you alone?"

Gwen's chin came up. "He felt my tagging along was too dangerous, that he couldn't protect me. He went off on his own to find the elusive bad guys and see that justice is served."

Colin had a point. If David really had been killed and the two of them were walking around in harm's way, knocking on unknown doors, then maybe Gwen really wasn't safe with Colin. Rowan felt a begrudging respect for his brother, surprised Colin had the maturity to put Gwen's safety above his own lustful concerns. "That was probably a good idea, Gwen."

She stopped next to an orange Suzuki and opened the passenger side door. "And why is that a good idea, exactly?"

He squinted at the driver of the car, unable to see beyond the glare on the windshield. "We don't want you to get hurt."

"We?" she asked, raising an eyebrow. "I see. I am no more fragile than you are, Rowan Mitchell. I'm a better shot with a weapon and I am well versed in the martial arts."

He took in her graceful limbs and feminine frame, doubting her ability to fend off a sixth grader.

Gwen put a hand on her hip. "Don't let my girlish good looks fool you."

He chuckled in spite of himself and climbed into the backseat of the car, surprised to see masses of red curly hair on the woman behind the wheel. The car smelled like cinnamon and something spicy, and the redhead turned toward him.

"I'm Becky."

"Rowan. Pleasure to meet you," he said, extending his hand.

"Not so fast, slick," said Becky. "Gwen and I are in this,

whether you like it or not. We're coming with you to find the bastard who killed Gwen's husband, and if you try to stop us I'm going to open a can of whoop-ass. You got that?"

Her eyes were incredible, a natural green that captivated him and drew him into their depths. Rowan was instantly aware of her, like he hadn't been aware of a woman in years. His eyes fell briefly to her lips, and returned to those eyes. "Whoop-ass?" he said, the lightest smile pulling at his mouth.

She raised her brows and moved her head from side to side. "Whoop-ass!"

"Got it."

"We do this together," said Becky.

Rowan nodded. "Whatever you say."

Gwen leaned her head back and peeked at Rowan. "Becky has a way with words."

"I can see that."

Becky held two cell phones in her hands, clearly copying a number from one to the other, then passed one to him. "You're calling Colin. It's ringing. Tell him you rented a car and find out where he is."

Rowan had the odd sense that he'd been kidnapped and was being held against his will. It rang several times before going to voicemail.

"It's Rowan. I just landed at Logan. Call me back at this number when you get this. My regular phone doesn't work in the States."

"Damn it," said Becky. "Where do we go now?"

"We go to Aunt Bernice's house. Six twenty-two Balina Place," said Gwen.

Becky backed out of the parking space. "Where'd you get that?"

"It was in the documents I was looking at with Colin yesterday morning."

"Good memory, girl."

"Actually, it's quite a coincidence. Six twenty-two is my anniversary—June twenty-second—and we went to Bali on our honeymoon."

Becky's slammed on the brake. "Are you kidding me?"

Gwen's eyes twinkled. "Don't you just love when things like that happen?"

Chapter 13

The disappearance of Emma Walker was newsworthy for a short period of time in the summer of 2001, wedged between the arrest of a serial arsonist and a scandal involving a small town sheriff's affection for child pornography.

Images of Emma's newly-rented apartment flooded the New York City suburban media for several days before the court of public opinion decreed she had likely left of her own volition. She was, after all, nearly twenty years old, and had recently broken up with her boyfriend. He was interviewed on channel six, telling the world that Emma longed for bigger and better things, and that he, for one, was unconcerned as to her whereabouts.

Colin had interviewed the boyfriend, though he had no legal authority to do so. The U.S. Marshal's Office had no interest in the disappearance of Graham Walker's daughter, but Colin certainly did. He clearly remembered the older man's devastation, a vacant look that haunted him as he sat at his desk and stared at nothing for what seemed like months. One minute Walker would be there, appearing to be engaged in his work—a meeting or paperwork—and the next he'd be gone, not to return for hours or even days on end.

The conversation with the boyfriend convinced Colin he knew nothing about Emma's disappearance, and despite Colin's best investigative efforts, the case soon disappeared off the radar of every legitimate agency.

That was when Walker really got bad. His clothes hung off his body, the collars of his shirts loose and awkward around his neck like so much knotted rope. His skin was ruddy and pale, his once-sharp eyes watery and bloodshot. Colin wondered if it was booze or sheer exhaustion, a lack of hope, that had gotten to the older man and destroyed his spirit.

Then came the day Colin stepped into Walker's office and was startled to see an older woman with short dark hair. "Where's Walker?" he asked.

She took off stylish reading glasses and eyed him frankly. "He's taken a leave of absence."

Walker lived for the job, had been good at it before his daughter vanished. He had run this department like his own personal kingdom, and it was unsettling to see anyone else sitting behind the big dark desk. Colin narrowed his eyes. "His request, or yours?"

"That's not for me to say."

"When's he coming back?"

"It's an indefinite leave. Perhaps you should contact him directly."

Colin tried. He called repeatedly, sent email messages like he was throwing rocks into a lake. He'd gone to Walker's house, only to find the old white colonial deserted. Colin stood in the driveway of his mentor's Connecticut home, taking in the peeling paint, the overgrown grass. Years earlier, Colin had stood in this exact same spot and thought what a lucky man Graham Walker was—the father of two beautiful children with a gorgeous house and a loving wife.

Now Walker's son was dead, crashing his motocycle into a tree with a blood alcohol level .21, Emma had vanished, and Walker's wife was living in an assisted care facility, though the reason she needed such help had never been offered. Perhaps the happy household was not what it seemed, or maybe it was simply a tragedy. Everything Walker cared about was gone.

Three months after Walker's sudden leave of absence, he returned just as unexpectedly.

"You're back," said Colin.

"Yes."

Colin took in Walker's straight posture, the clear eyes. "Anything on Emma?"

Walker didn't even blink. "She's not coming back."

"Is she…"

"She's fine, Mitchell," he bit out. "She has her own life now."

Colin nodded, understanding he would not be given an explanation. "I'm glad you're back, sir."

~~~

Gwen stepped to the door of Jerry's aunt Bernice's house and rang the bell, taking in her surroundings as she waited. The neighborhood of small brick ranches was welcoming and quaint, with small square yards and mature shrubs and trees. An elderly woman at the house next door was watching her, and Gwen waved pleasantly, earning her a nod and a smile.

The door opened to a tall young man with warm brown skin.

"Hi there, my name's Gwen Trueblood. I'm hoping you can help me find someone."

The man was happy to help, but he had never heard of Jerry or his aunt, telling Gwen his parents had lived in the house for the past nine years.

Gwen slid back into the passenger seat of Becky's car and reached for the seat belt. "No luck." She shook her head. "I thought for sure we were going to find out where Jerry is." Gwen's intuition rarely steered her wrong, and she was nonplussed, unsure of what to do next.

"Wait for it," said Becky, pulling her sunglasses down and peering over Gwen's shoulder. The woman from next door walked gingerly toward them.

"Hello," said Gwen.

"Are you looking for Bernice?"

Gwen nodded. "I am! Her nephew, actually. He's my father-in-law."

"Oh dear, I'm so sorry," the woman's face fell. "You're looking for Jerry?"

"Yes."

"He passed away years ago, my dear."

Jerry was dead? Gwen didn't realize just how much she was looking forward to meeting David's father until the possibility disappeared. "Oh."

"I'm sorry to be the one to tell you." She sighed heavily. "Jerry got himself into a little trouble and he went into Witness Protection. It was a few years after that he passed away."

Gwen was confused. Was she referring to the dead Jerry of Cold spring, who was never really dead at all, or the true death of the man sometime later?

"Bernice," said the old woman, "moved out to Sandwich to

live with her son and his wife, must be upwards of ten years now. She needed a little help to get along when she got the cancer."

"Sandwich?" asked Gwen, the hair rising on her arms as she remembered Martin's story.

Becky leaned close to Gwen, sticking her head close to the window. "Do you know where we can find her son?"

"Why, yes. A little place down the road from the boardwalk entrance. A gray house with white shutters. If you find the boardwalk, you can't miss it."

~~~

The boardwalk cut through marshlands and over inlets, the grasses providing no cover to someone who wanted to remain inconspicuous. James McDonald turned his collar up against the wind and tucked his chin inside the jacket.

He only had one chance to get this right.

His stomach hadn't stopped churning since that fateful phone call. He had packed a change of clothes and the unregistered Glock he'd been given years ago by his partner when the older man retired. You never know when you might need it, he had said. James had laughed, unable to imagine any such scenario.

Until now.

He walked along the wooden planks toward the beach, the sound of his footfalls like a ticking clock, marking the moments before he would pull the trigger. His fingers gingerly checked the safety on the weapon in the large pocket of his windbreaker, the shake of his hand alarming. Would he be steady enough to take the shot when he got there?

His feet stopped moving beneath him and he twisted around, eyeing the path that led back to his car. The wooden boards stretched out for what looked like miles, straight and still amid the blowing grasses. He could walk back to the car, leave this place behind forever.

He'd have to leave everything. His wife, his child. Go on the run. He could never be free that way, never be sure they were all right.

What looked like escape might really be the road to certain

death. He turned back around, the ocean now visible at the horizon. If he did what he came here to do, things could go back to the way they were. Yes, there might be another call. But there could also be another twelve-year reprieve. There had been so many good years, so much happiness between those two phone calls. His feet began to move again.

James wanted things back the way they were, before he ran for mayor, before he became sheriff, even. He wanted to be broke again, eating hot dogs and drinking beer with Jeannie in front of the TV in their little house by the river. Christ, when was the last time they'd even sat down next to each other on the couch, no less touched each other like they used to back then, all horny and wild?

Sand began to rain down like hail and he realized he was crying, the grains sticking to his face as he tried to wipe them away. He cried for what he was about to do, for the woman he loved and had married, for the son he might never see again, and the wretched hole in his soul that had allowed this horror to happen.

Chapter 14

Gwen didn't believe in worrying. It served only to magnify negative energy that would otherwise pass her by. So when she found herself concerned for Colin on the drive to Sandwich Beach, she gave the sensation due note and raised her head in silent prayer.

Be with him. Keep him safe.

Her heart was filled with such longing to have him by her side that the emotion gave her pause. Had she so easily become attached to the man that she was somehow incomplete without him, like a vacuum to be filled instead of a solid rock to stand on? Her brow furrowed as she watched homes slip by the speeding car, cruising toward Sandwich Beach.

Gwen hoped Becky was right, that the son living there was really Jerry. It was certainly possible Bernice found it easier to kill off her nephew than live in the shadow of his crimes, just as David himself had done. The thought of living in one's shadow brought her back to Colin, her conflicting emotions warring inside her.

Gwen deeply valued her independence, her own personality and strength of character. While she had given herself completely to her husband, her quick identification as Colin's lover was more troublesome. She was not a person who loved in degrees, yet this time she couldn't help but feel she would be losing something important, something she had never considered she was losing when she married David.

Herself.

In the years since her husband died, Gwen had become something more than she had been when he was by her side. She had become more fully herself, more comfortable alone than she could ever be with Colin. She tapped her fingers on the car door in a staccato rhythm.

Something else was bothering her, too. Colin had left her behind in consideration for her safety. While she wanted to understand that, what struck her most was that he did not see her as an equal, capable partner—an asset. His actions showed he thought her a liability, a responsibility, a problem to be handled.

Such was not love. At least, it was not love as Gwen experienced it.

The feminine in her spirit admitted it had hurt her to awaken to an empty room. She and Colin had shared something magical, the sort of connection that was reserved for the most special relationships in life.

But it couldn't be love. It made sense she should care for Colin. He'd been a player in an important part of her life, a time that she cherished and longed to revisit. Could she blame herself for falling so willingly into his arms? For enjoying the man and the sexual chemistry between them?

Colin had always mistaken what they shared for something deeper. He claimed an awareness of her while they'd been separated that she just didn't share. The truth was, Gwen had rarely thought of Colin in the years since she'd last seen him. She shifted in her seat, bristling at what she knew was an exaggeration. Yes, she had frequently thought of Colin, but had blocked the sensations out of lingering guilt over David. Maybe there'd been wisdom in that.

Rowan interrupted her thoughts. "Gwen, something's been bothering me, and I'm just going to ask, okay?" he said.

"Of course." She turned around in her seat to face him, pushing her sunglasses atop her head.

"Last night when I called Colin and you answered, you said he was in the shower."

She instantly saw where this was going. "Yes?"

"How did you know that?"

"I could hear the water running."

"Because you were sharing a room."

She faced forward. "And you don't approve."

Becky piped up. "What business is it of yours if they shared a room?"

"I was talking to Gwen."

"I don't care who you were talking to. You asked the question in front of me, so clearly you wanted me to hear it. And it just so happens I have an opinion about this matter that I'd like to share."

"Oh, yeah? What's that?"

Becky yelled. "Mind your own goddamn business, Mitchell."

"It is my business."

Gwen couldn't believe his self-righteousness. He was treating her like a child, not unlike how his brother had treated her just this morning, and she was ticked. "How do you figure my sex life is any of your concern?"

"So, you admit you slept with him."

Becky shook her hand at the rearview mirror as she drove. "Someone needs to pound you in the face."

"Rowan, you are out of line," said Gwen.

"He's been after you since day one, back when you were with David, hitting on you all the time. It's not right."

Gwen could hear the pain in his voice, and suddenly realized the problem. Rowan's anger with Colin was a façade for a different emotion, one that she understood all too well. Grief took whatever shape it was allowed, often eking out when least expected. "David is gone."

"I know that, but how do you think he would feel about you and Colin…" he shrugged his shoulder, "being together?"

"He wants me to be happy." Gwen's eyes began to burn as she stared at her husband's oldest friend. "He wants you to be happy, too. He doesn't want you to hold on to this grief, this pain you feel from his death, and let it ruin your relationship with the brother who is very much alive."

She could see by his expression that her words had hit their mark.

"Colin makes you happy?"

Gwen faced forward and gazed out her window, considering her response.

Becky smacked her arm. "Answer the man!"

"Oh, I don't know. I'm still trying to figure that out for myself."

~~~

Rowan stretched out his long legs on the seat beside him. The backseat of Becky's car wasn't made for a man his size. He stared at her vibrant hair, knowing now that it matched an equally vibrant personality. She was a woman who could keep a man on his toes, and he found himself wondering about the lucky bastard who got to share her bed.

They must be lining up in droves.

She was too young for him, anyway. At forty-three, Rowan wasn't interested in dating a woman who must be at least fifteen years his junior. It occurred to him that not a lot of women wanted to date a married man, and he thought again of the divorce lawyer's business card in his pocket. It was long past time to make that phone call.

He put his hands behind his head and tried to stretch out. The flight was long and he hadn't slept well on the plane, too concerned about Colin and Gwen getting it on in a hotel room to close his eyes for more than an hour or two. He sighed. Gwen seemed to think he was upset with Colin because David was dead, not because Colin was interested in Gwen. The thought let an unpleasant taste in his mouth, though he could hear the lightest ring of truth in her words when she spoke them.

Rowan was still mourning his best friend, simple as that. He looked out the window and wondered if he would ever be able to accept Gwen and Colin being together. He doubted it, that was for sure.

The cell phone on his lap began to ring.

Rowan answered the phone. "Hello."

Colin's voice was harsh. "You're here?"

Rowan wasn't expecting a warm and fuzzy welcome, yet Colin's tone hurt nonetheless. Too many years had passed since he'd been close to his brother, too much foul water running under that bridge. "I couldn't let you do this by yourself. I flew in overnight, got a rental car."

"It's not your responsibility."

"He belonged to both of us, Colin."

A pause on the line had Rowan holding his breath. In that moment, he missed his brother desperately. Missed the relationship they used to have, long before the issue with Gwen had thrown a wedge between them. Rowan half expected his brother to tell him to get back on a plane and head for Italy.

Colin sighed heavily. "Okay. Thanks."

Rowan closed his eyes. "You got it. Now where the hell are you?"

Chapter 15

Colin walked along the boardwalk as gulls screeched overhead. There was a bench, right where he was told it would be, and he sat down to wait.

He could feel Gwen's spirit, worried for him, and reveled in their connection. She claimed she didn't feel it, but how could that be? Was it possible such a thing could ever be one-sided?

Memories of last night flashed through his mind. In the stress of the day and the hunt for Ahearn, Colin hadn't allowed himself the luxury of remembering his lovemaking with Gwen. Now he bathed in the images, subtle scents and sensations that swarmed him, wrapping around him like an all-consuming blanket.

It had been better than any fantasy, more intense than he could have imagined. Gwen Trueblood had touched him, body and soul, like no woman before her ever had. He could hardly wait to do it again.

She's going to be mad as all hell.

He reached up to rub at his neck. He knew the woman well enough to know there would be repercussions for his actions this morning, he didn't care as long as she was safe.

The sound of the surf seemed to intensify, one mother earth defending another. Colin's eyes were drawn to the horizon, the wind-whipped water reflecting the bright sunshine of a cloudless summer day. A heron appeared, tiny at first, gliding gracefully to the water and swooping low to catch a fish in the shallow water.

Colin turned his head toward a movement down the boardwalk. It was a man, head bent against the blowing sand, his gait a familiar stride that clawed at Colin's heartstrings. The recognition surprised him. This was Jerry Ahearn, David's father. Colin had been a young child the last time he saw Jerry, yet still he remembered.

Time dangled as the man approached, finally reaching the bench and sitting down so lightly that the seat barely moved beneath him. His posture was stooped, his jacket lightly pulling at his paunch. "It's been a long time, Mitchell."

The voice was familiar, too. More like David's than he remembered. Colin took in Jerry's wrinkled eyes, the gray and white hair atop his head, the pale fingers. Mentally he juxtaposed this old man with the beautiful Emma, her radiant youth only making Jerry seem older.

What had she seen in this man, that she would abandon her life and her family?

Jerry shook his head. "You're all grown up, Mitchell."

"I am. So you must be what, mid-sixties?"

He nodded.

"But your wife is only thirty."

"Emma said she explained."

"Maybe you can explain it better."

He cleared his throat. "The boy isn't mine, Mitchell. Emma was pregnant before I met her."

"Who's the father?"

He shrugged. "I never asked her. It didn't matter to me."

"You were in love and that's all that mattered? I'm not buying it, Jerry." He narrowed his eyes harshly. "Too much of a coincidence. I'm looking for the man who killed your son, and I run into my boss's long lost daughter, who just happens to be your wife. Don't you find that–"

Jerry grabbed his arm. "Killed my son?" His mouth worked. "David was murdered?"

Damn it. He'd forgotten that Jerry didn't know. "I believe so. I'm sorry, Jerry."

Jerry sank back on the bench, his jaw slack.

Colin wanted to feel sorry for this man, but all he could conjure was blame. Jerry could have sold cars, or worked construction, and David and his mother would be alive right now. Jerry was responsible for every tragedy that befell his family. He made a choice to engage in organized crime, he turned state's evidence, and he couldn't stay clean.

"They said it was a skiing accident."

"That's what we thought." Colin chastised himself again for not interviewing Gwen himself at the time. He knew now it was cowardice that had kept him away. "David recognized someone on the mountain that day. Someone from his childhood named Michael."

Jerry frowned. "Michael Gallente?"

"I was hoping you could tell me. David said it was someone he went to school with."

"They both went to Holy Cross. They were friends. That's the only Michael I remember."

"You testified against his father." Colin couldn't keep the accusation out of his voice. His own life's work was seeing that those who testified were kept safe, yet here and now, when it was his friend who had paid the ultimate price, he hated Jerry for what he had done.

"I thought we'd be safe, protected. Or I never would have done it."

"In WITSEC."

"Yes." He shook his head. "But we were betrayed."

Betrayed. Bullshit, they were betrayed. Colin had heard it before in his role as U.S. Marshal. It was a failure to take responsibility for your own actions, an inability to accept that you had created the very mess that worked to destroy you. "Adele was unhappy. She contacted her mother," said Colin.

Jerry's gaze was sharp. "What do you know about it?"

Reaching into his back pocket, Colin extracted his wallet and showed Jerry his badge. The other man met his eyes accusingly.

"Talk about your coincidences," said Jerry.

"What do you mean?"

"I go to prison, and the grandson of the woman who takes custody of my boy becomes a U.S. Marshal."

"I became a Marshal because I wanted to help people like David. He lived with us after you went back to prison. It wasn't a coincidence at all."

Jerry sighed. "You'll forgive me if I'm not impressed."

"I don't forgive you for shit, Ahearn. I don't forgive you for the crimes that put you in WITSEC, I don't forgive you for the death of your wife, and I don't forgive you for the death of my friend or the grief of his widow."

Jerry jabbed at him with his finger. "You ride in here on

your high horse and think you know everything. Well, you don't know a goddamn thing, Mitchell. You've swallowed anything they put in front of you, hook, line and sinker."

A sudden cold breeze whipped off the water. "I don't have time for this crap," said Colin.

"Graham Walker killed my wife."

Colin opened his hands, flexed his fingers. His own lack of faith in Walker wouldn't allow him to defend the man, and he hated himself for it. "Your wife killed herself when she contacted her mother. You can't put that on Walker or anyone else, except maybe yourself. If you hadn't lived the life you led, forced her to leave her family behind, she wouldn't have been in that situation in the first place."

Jerry stood. "She didn't contact her mother. Walker made that up after he shot her."

"I don't believe that."

"Let me guess, he's a friend of yours." Jerry spit on the ground. "They were having an affair, Mitchell. From the time I first entered the program."

"How do you know?"

"My wife was pregnant, but she hadn't slept with me in almost a year."

Colin's heart stopped beating. Adele wasn't even two months along when she died. Jerry couldn't have known she was expecting unless she told him herself.

Or could he?

Had someone told Jerry about the coroner's report? Someone on the inside? Colin's thoughts reeled. He needed time to think, to sort out this new information.

An image formed in Colin's mind of Graham Walker and Adele Ahearn. Was it possible? The young deputy and the gangster's wife, caught in a love affair that could only end badly?

If Jerry was correct, Walker could have lost everything—his career, his wife. He might have been desperate, and desperate people did desperate things. Colin bit the inside of his cheek. "Go on."

"I went to see her at the beauty shop where she worked.

We'd been fighting since she told me about the affair." He hung his head. "She wanted to leave me, take David with her and be with Walker. I was tired of it, defeated. I told her she could go to him if she wanted."

"Walker was going to leave June for her?" Colin pictured Mrs. Walker, beautiful and ever devoted to her husband. He couldn't imagine Walker ever choosing someone else over her.

Jerry shook his head slowly. "That was what she wanted, but he didn't want her. He said he never loved her, that he wouldn't leave his wife, and wanted Adele to get rid of the baby. He was coming to give her the money that day, but she didn't want to do it. She was hysterical, crying like a little kid." He wiped at his eye with the back of his hand.

"She begged me—begged me—to forgive her. She said we could keep the baby and no one would ever know it wasn't mine, that she'd be a good wife to me again." His face crumpled as he let out a sob. He shook his head quickly. "I told her no. No way. My pride was so hurt. I wasn't going to raise that bastard's child." Tears fell unchecked down his face.

"I didn't leave her a choice, don't you see? She needed me and I turned her away. She hustles me out the door, says he's coming. She's going to convince him they can make it work with the baby." Jerry pressed his lips together into a tight line. "Two hours later, I get a phone call from Walker. She's dead. He tells me she contacted her mother, someone walked into the shop and killed her, but I knew the truth."

Colin listened to Jerry's quiet sobbing as he watched as an orange car pull into a parking lot some hundred yards away. "Did you tell anyone what you're telling me now?"

"Hell no."

"Why not?"

Jerry crossed his feet and tucked them under the bench, his body huddled against the cold wind. "David."

The single word spoke volumes.

"It was just him and me, now. I was all he had…" his voice cracked and he cleared his throat. "Walker was my contact at WITSEC. If he suspected I knew about Adele, I'd be dead, either by his gun or with a simple slip of the tongue. I had to stay alive to take care of my son. I couldn't touch Walker."

Colin wanted to say he was wrong, that there were enough checks and balances to keep any one man from having such power, yet he knew Jerry spoke the truth. To him, Walker was omnipotent, untouchable. But Jerry had managed to find Walker's Achilles heel, his singular weakness. "Until Emma."

Jerry nodded, taking a deep breath and exhaling slowly. "I didn't plan it."

A flock of seagulls landed on the beach, squawking. In the distance, a man walked toward them on the boardwalk. Colin thought of Walker, the man who represented authority and patriotism and integrity. He wanted to say Jerry was lying, but the story he told held a ring of truth that resonated deep in the pit of Colin's stomach.

"I came to see Walker when I got out of prison. I waited outside his office to talk to him and I could hear him fighting with Emma. He told her to get rid of it, and she was crying so hard…" His eyes met Colin's, their depths clear and bright. "Don't you see? It was my chance. My chance to make everything right."

"Your chance to get back at Walker."

"Yes. But I could take care of Emma, give her a safe place to have her baby." His chin quivered. "I could do for her what I didn't do for Adele."

Colin turned away, staring at the horizon. It was incredible. Two worlds had overlapped, usurping an entire person from one world and placing her in another. "She stayed with you all these years."

"We care about each other. We've raised a child together."

"Are you telling me you're in love?"

His smiled slightly. "As much as a beautiful young woman can ever be in love with an old man like me. I've done my best to be a good husband to her. The boy has been a joy." A shadow crossed Jerry's features. "Just like my David, even if Luke doesn't share my blood."

"One more question, Jerry."

"Yeah?"

"Why'd you go to Walker's office that day?"

The loud crack of a gunshot ripped across the beach. Blood appeared on Jerry's chest and Colin hit the ground like a dead man.

Chapter 16

Gwen watched in terror as Colin fell to the ground, the import of the loud bang only now registering on her consciousness. "Colin!" she screamed, the wrenching sound of her voice like a stranger's as she reached for the door handle and moved to get out.

"Stay in the car!" Becky grabbed Gwen's arm and yanked her back to the seat.

"I have to help him!"

Rowan was frantically unzipping his luggage. "I have a gun. I have a gun." He pulled it out and continued rifling through the bag. "Bullets. Bullets. Shit!" He found the box and loaded the weapon quickly.

Why did Rowan have a gun?

Gwen held out her hand. "Give it to me."

"No."

"I'm a better shot than you are!"

Rowan stared back at her, frozen with indecision. Another shot rang out along the beach.

"Give me the fucking gun!" Gwen yelled.

He slapped it into her hand and she was out the door, running toward the scene on the boardwalk, weapon drawn. The noise of the surf covered her footfalls as she quickly cut the distance in half and the shooter advanced on the bench, his back still to her.

Jerry was slumped at an unnatural angle, unmoving, but Colin was now behind the bench and Jerry's eerily still form. He must have moved there when she was getting the gun.

Close enough now to get off a shot, she stopped running and trained her weapon at the shooter just as he rounded the bench toward Colin and saw her.

Gwen pulled the trigger, her destiny hanging in the balance as the bullets made their way across the sand-covered boardwalk. The instant became a moment that stretched out and held, seagulls squawking in the distance, allowing her a glimpse at what might come to be.

She could see herself and Colin, sitting on the porch swing at her house, love a living presence between them. She felt the warmth of sunshine on her arm as if she was really sitting there, and a contentedness in her heart like she'd never before experienced.

His brown eyes laughed into hers and she smiled. A breeze blew so sharply that she turned around, Colin disappearing in an instant. The sunshine still warmed her skin on a glorious summer day, but Gwen was alone on the swing, gently rocking. David stood before her on the porch.

"What do you want, Gwen?" he asked.

"I want Colin," she whispered, her heart singing with the admission. "I want to be a wife again. I want to be a mother."

David smiled at her, and she was filled with understanding. Her story would continue, and continue to be attached to and honor this man, even as she came to love another.

The warmth of the sunshine turned hotter and hotter, becoming a searing heat that burned her arm. Gwen looked down and saw blood, then raised her head to watch the shooter fall backwards to the ground. Then Becky was there, saying something, and Rowan ran to the bench to check on his brother's unmoving form.

~~~

The boy looked just like Walker's son Tommy had at ten. He was lean and tan, with tousled brown hair that fell in his face when he bent to weed the garden. Walker lifted his cell phone so the camera lens just peeked over the door of the car and took a picture, knowing that the distance would make it difficult for him to see the boy at all.

Ahearn had done this, taken his family away. Walker didn't even know his grandson's name. Blame was absolute and powerful, bitterness rising up in Walker's gut to eat away at any tenderness that once lived there.

An image of his Emma rose up in his memory, her body heavy with pregnancy as she screamed at him. He had thought her grotesque, disfigured, having never expected her to keep the child he was so eager to forget.

"Get away from me! I hate you!" she yelled.

Walker had staked out Emma's best friend's house for weeks on end, knowing how hard it was to sever all ties to a former life. "It's time to come home and stop this foolishness, Emma. You've won. You get to keep your bastard."

"I'm never coming home." She held her chin high in the air.

"Where will you go? How will you support yourself?"

Her eyes gleamed as she delivered the blow. "I'm with Jerry Ahearn now, Dad."

Walker paled.

"He takes care of me. He loves this baby and he loves me."

Had that bastard touched his daughter? Dear God. Was that his baby? An image appeared in his mind and he forcibly pushed it back. "Ahearn's a monster. A murderer. You have to know that."

"Well, look at the pot calling the kettle black." She stepped toward him. "I know what you did, Daddy. You cheated on mom with Jerry's wife, then you killed Adele so she wouldn't have your baby."

He longed to cover her mouth with his hand, stop the filthy stream of words coming out. Secrets long buried rose up and danced, tormenting him. It occurred to him that Emma couldn't be trusted with his secret, that he had to stop her from leaving here, from ruining everything. There was only one way to do that, to keep himself safe. His fingers trembled.

Emma's face was snarled in disgust. "You killed your lover and your own child, like you tried to get me to kill mine." A single tear ran down her face and she swiped at it with the back of her hand. The movement was intimately familiar to him, something he had seen her do hundreds of times growing up. He stepped back, frightened by what he'd been considering. "What do you want from me?" he whispered.

"Stay away from us, or I'll tell everyone what you did."

"You can't do that."

"Why not, Daddy? Are you going to kill me, too?"

The fact that he had been considering that very thing filled him with a special horror.

I've lost everyone I have ever loved.

Adele was dead, June was tucked away in a nursing home with barely a memory of her own name, his daughter hated him and his son was dead. Mitchell had been a substitute for so many things in his life, and now he had turned on him too, left him alone to face his own demons by himself.

Walker watched as the boy raked up debris from the garden. There would be no relationship with him, no Christmas dinners or drawings made just for grandpa. Walker gripped his gun in his hand and for the first time considered using it on himself. The weight of the cold metal was an odd comfort, a choice that needed to be made. Colin was the final antagonist of Walker's life, Colin's defection the last chapter.

Walker released the safety, just as his phone began to ring, pulling him from his soliloquy.

"Hello?"

"It's Michael. Long time no see."

Chapter 17

Rowan stepped out of the hospital elevator and saw Becky at a vending machine, the curves of her body held tightly in a pair of equally curvy jeans. She bent to retrieve a bag of chips and he felt like a randy teenager.

He cleared his throat. "Hey."

A package of licorice fell from its perch. "Hey yourself."

"How's Gwen?"

She inserted a dollar bill and sipped at a Hawaiian Punch. "Good. The gunshot was purely superficial." A pair of cupcakes dropped. "She'll have a scar on her arm, but they didn't even admit her." She began feeding coins into the slot.

"Hungry?" he asked.

"Why, you want something?" A chocolate bar landed with a thud.

Did he ever. A certain redhead with the appetite of a horse. "No, I'm good." He shifted his weight. "Have you seen Colin yet?"

"He's still in post-op. They got the bullet."

"Good. Good. They say anything else?"

She took a swig of her drink. "Nope."

Rowan stared at her lips, full and unnaturally red from the punch.

"You sure you're not hungry?" she asked, putting one hand on her hip. "Because you're looking at me like you're starving."

Lust shot through him at her brazen words, her eyes challenging. "Sorry."

"Right." She took another sip, slowly turning and walking beside him, her arm lightly brushing his. "So, you live in Italy?"

"Yeah."

"How'd you end up over there?"

He cocked his head, seeing the brick wall that he was about to run into, but unable to slow down the vehicle. "I followed a woman."

"Ah, I see. How did that work out?"

"We got married."

"Married?"

He nodded, his face grim.

"Wait, you're married?"

He wanted to explain, but as he imagined the wretched story falling from his lips and her inevitable reaction, he changed his mind. "I am." *Crash.*

She raised her eyebrows but said nothing. Maybe it was just as well. He certainly couldn't get into a relationship right now with everything such a mess back at home. Rowan knew he had to deal with it, face facts and move on, but some things were easier said than done.

"Tell me something," Becky said.

"Shoot."

"What do you have against Colin and Gwen being together?"

"He was after her years ago, before she and David were even married."

"So?"

"So, he was totally out of line. He had no respect for Gwen or David, who was like a brother to both of us. It was messed up."

"Okay." She crossed her arms over her chest. "But that was years ago. He was a kid. Now David's dead and Colin and Gwen want to be together."

He bristled at her easy use of the word dead, as if he was an obstacle that was easily removed. "Really? Is that what Gwen wants?"

Becky's mouth moved to one side as she considered. "It's what she really wants, deep down."

"Says who, you?"

She rolled her eyes. "Fine. Let me rephrase that. If—" she stressed, "they want to be together, then who the hell are you to try and stop them?"

"I'm his brother."

"Well, duh."

"There are a million woman he can have. Why does he have to chase the one who got away, the only one in the whole wide world that it kills me to see him with?"

"We love who we love."

"He could find someone else."

"Oh, because we women are totally interchangeable, right?"

He sneered, getting flustered. "That's not what I said."

"Sure it is. But regardless, Colin wants Gwen. He doesn't want any of those other women." She let her eyes scan the length of him. "I know some men have eyes for lots of different girls, but men of character tend to pick one and stick with it."

Rowan knew damn well she was talking about him, and he didn't like it one bit. He was not about to explain himself to this woman who thought she knew everything. She had already put him inside a little box and scrawled "cheater" across the lid. He ran his hand through his hair. "I'm going to see if Colin can have visitors yet."

He wandered back to the nurse's station by the elevator. "Is Colin Mitchell out of post-op yet? I'd like to see him."

"And you are?"

"His brother."

She typed in a computer. "He's not awake yet, but you can go in. Room 318, just past the drinking fountain."

Rowan stepped into the room and saw his brother lying still on the bed. The seriousness of the situation hit him again, his agitation with his brother all but forgotten. Colin's arm was tightly wrapped and bound to his torso in type of sling, an IV in his other arm and several monitors working at his bedside.

Some things were more important than who Colin dated. Like whether or not he was alive. Rowan put his hands in his pockets and walked to the window. This day could have ended very differently, and he was filled with gratitude for their good fortune.

Footsteps behind him and he turned to see Gwen, looking uncharacteristically sporty in a pair of jeans and a Boston Red Sox t-shirt. Her eyes followed his down her outfit. "My clothes had blood on them."

Of course. She'd been injured, could have been killed, while he sat in the car and watched. Despite his wounded pride, he knew it had been the right decision. "I couldn't have made that shot," he said.

"Yes, well…" her voice trailed off. "The shooter. Is he alive?"

He could hear the hope in her voice, and hated to be the one to crush it. "He died in surgery."

She nodded, staring at a spot on the wall. "I figured as much."

"You did what you had to do, Gwen."

"Did they find out who he was?"

"James McDonald."

"Why is that name familiar to me?"

"He's the sheriff of your town in Vermont. He was running for mayor."

"You've got to be kidding me." She sank down on the edge of Colin's bed and covered her hand with her mouth. "He was there the day David was killed, on the mountain. He interviewed me!"

"Maybe he killed David."

She shook her head. "I don't understand. David recognized someone named Michael that day, someone from his childhood. What are the chances of that happening, and someone else being the killer?"

"Maybe it's a coincidence."

"In my experience, the universe works very hard to provide us with the information we need. To call it a coincidence is to laugh in the face of the divine's most dramatic intervention."

"So who the hell is Michael?"

"I don't know, but I'm going to find out."

~~~

Colin could feel the weight of his arm, splinted across his chest, and remembered. He was on his knees on the sand-covered boardwalk, blood splattered on the ground. He couldn't get to his weapon, concealed on the same side of his body as his injured arm, and he flung himself behind the bench and Jerry's slumped form in search of cover from their attacker.

Gwen. The thought crossed his mind like a prayer. She had been there, running toward them, weapon drawn. Was Gwen okay?

Colin worked to open his eyes, the hospital room coming into focus. She sat beside him, doing a crossword puzzle with a pen, and relief flooded his senses. "Hi." His voice was hoarse and didn't sound like his own.

Concern filled her eyes. "How are you feeling?" she asked, reaching for his hand.

"Like I went ten rounds with Mike Tyson."

Gwen smiled softly. "I'm so glad you're okay."

"What happened?"

She filled him in on the events at the beach and the identity of the shooter. The sheriff was dead, but Jerry was hanging in there.

"Thank God you're a good shot."

"We all have our gifts."

His mind worked to absorb everything she had told him. "McDonald must have been working for someone."

"Someone who knew who David really was."

Colin frowned. "Someone like Graham Walker." Betrayal seeped through him. Any doubt he had about Jerry's story vanished like so much smoke in the breeze. His mentor really was guilty, and Colin had to stop him before he was able to hurt any more people. "I need to get the hell out of this hospital room."

"What are we going to do?" asked Gwen.

His protective instincts reared up and he eyed her warily.

"Colin Mitchell, don't you dare try to leave me behind again. You underestimated my value once already and it nearly cost you your life. I am vital to your wellbeing, like vitamins or sunlight."

He gave an appreciative chuckle. She was more important that either of those things. "How did you find me?"

"Rowan. We picked him up at the airport."

"Where is he now?"

"With Becky in the cafeteria."

"I'm going to need his help. And yours, too."

"Are we going to find Walker?"

He shook his head. "I'm sure he's already here. We just need to tell him exactly where to find us."

Chapter 18

Rowan pulled under the portico of the hotel and put the car in park.

"Be right back," said Becky, as she and Gwen hopped out of the backseat and disappeared into the hotel lobby. Colin sat beside him, the tension between the brothers seeming to stretch on interminably.

As the oldest, Rowan was used to being in charge, used to being the authority, used to being right. It was hard for him to see when he was wrong, and even harder for him to apologize and make peace with Colin. He shifted uncomfortably in his seat. "How's your arm?"

"It hurts like a son-of-a-bitch. Why?"

"Could be worse. I'm glad you're not dead."

"I'm glad I'm not dead, too."

Rowan gripped the steering wheel. "Listen, about you and Gwen."

Colin sighed heavily. "Rowan, it's none of your business."

"I know."

"So then why the hell are we talking about it?"

"Because I'm sorry."

Colin narrowed his eyes. "Sorry for what?"

"For being upset about it earlier. For expecting you to act like she was still married to David even though he's gone."

"Thanks."

Rowan pointed his finger at Colin's chest. "It still wasn't okay, what you did back then."

"I know." Colin turned to stare after the women. "I'm sorry, too. It was selfish and wrong, and it cost me my relationship with David."

"How about we never talk about this again?"

"Deal."

Becky and Gwen climbed into the car.

"Pull around back and park by the blue door," said Gwen. "I got us a suite with a hot tub."

"I got a suite with a hot tub, too," said Becky.

"What about me?" Rowan asked her.

"I got you a studio."

"Were they all out of hot tubs?"

"Nope."

Rowan shook his head. She wasn't one for subtlety, was she? He parked the car and tried not to picture Becky up to her armpits in a sea of shiny bubbles.

"Walker's meeting me at Flynn's at noon," said Colin. "I think you three should go in an hour earlier, play it like you're tourists, eat some lunch."

"We only have the one car," said Rowan.

"I can take the T. It's a block from here and just up the street from the bar."

Rowan raised his eyebrows. "The cops took my gun as evidence in the shooting."

"Damn it." Colin smacked his hand to his forehead. "Becky?"

"Me?" she looked around. "I'm a democrat. There's pepper spray in the glove box."

Rowan chuckled. "It's better than nothing."

"Okay, everybody get some sleep. I have a feeling we're going to need it. We'll meet back here tomorrow morning at ten."

~~~

The suite consisted of a kitchenette and living room, with a separate bedroom and bath. Oddly, the hot tub was in the bedroom, right next to the king-size bed. Gwen had been looking forward to exploring its depths, but now found herself feeling awkward and shy.

Colin must have seen her discomfiture. "You can close the bedroom door if you want privacy."

"I wish you could join me," she said honestly.

His eyes darkened. "The bandages…"

"I know. I just wish."

"Me too." He reached for the bedroom door, pulling it closed behind him. "Enjoy your bath. I'll be here when you get out."

She nodded, grateful for the opportunity to relax in the water. She drew the bath piping hot, figured out how to turn on the jets, and added a tiny bottle of shampoo for bubbles before sinking into the tub. Her own wound was high on her arm, allowing her some freedom, and she rested her head along the back edge of the Jacuzzi like a cat stretching in the sun.

She loved that Colin was waiting for her, loved the lovemaking she was certain was coming. She loved the man himself, and the knowledge seeped into her bones like water seeping into the earth.

I love him.

Gwen was filled with the urge to create, to somehow describe with color and shape how this love lifted her up, made her whole where she had only been broken, made her sing where she had not had known the tune. Her mind went back to the painting of the storm, so meaningful now, the vibrant peacock green that was Colin Mitchell filling up her canvas as he now filled her mind.

The noise of the water jets became for her a roaring wind, an approaching thunder. They were indeed in the middle of a torrent, with evil very much alive and tormenting the new lovers. Tomorrow they would be in danger again, facing off the very forces that had conspired to take love from Gwen once before, whisking away her happiness like dried leaves in the breeze.

Would her love be safe this time, emerge victorious in the battle that had already claimed so many lives? Gwen's eyes closed tightly against her fears, her hands bouncing on the bubbles of air that forced their way to the surface. She wanted to believe she and Colin were ready to face the challenge ahead, prepared to pound evil into the ground and back to the very hell that had spawned it. But what if she was wrong? What if she would lose this man as well?

Sitting up in the bath, Gwen turned off the tap and the water jets. The room was suddenly quiet, the water still. Here in this moment, all was well with the world. Her love waited for her, time allowing them the gift of togetherness for another whole night. She would embrace it fully, disallowing the horror that lay outside these doors the opportunity to take love away from her again.

She called out to Colin, inviting him in. She stood to help him undress and bathed him slowly with a washcloth, savoring the brush of her arms along his skin. Gwen told him what was in her heart, his words of love rushing to meet her own, and they sank onto the bed to make love, enough love to last them a lifetime.

~~~

Graham Walker motioned to the bartender. "Another scotch on the rocks." He checked his watch, pushing his wrist farther away so he could make out the numbers. Nearly noon. He'd been here since ten thirty, waiting for this meeting with Colin like a condemned man waits on death row.

He made no attempt to survey the patrons in the bar, figuring that Mitchell had at least one person in the vicinity. His precious protégé would no doubt be hunkered down for war. Wouldn't he be surprised when he found only a drunken, broken old man, ready to confess his sins?

The thought left a bitter taste in his mouth and he gulped at his drink to chase it away. He was a man with limited options, his actions now dictated by another. Walker had laced the string to himself years before, never imagining it could one day be used to control him.

The noise of the street grew louder, and Walker turned to see Colin step into the bar. The sling was unexpected, and Walker was immediately concerned, feeling responsible. "What happened to you?" he asked.

Colin's stare was cool, and Walker's heart sank a little lower in his chest. It was one thing to suspect the other man had lost faith in him. It was another to see it clearly etched into his features. Walker signaled the bartender. "Glenlivet—"

Colin raised his hand. "Just a Coke."

A line in the sand. The first of several, Walker was sure. His fingers shook slightly as he reached for his drink. May as well get right to it. "Why didn't you call me after the fire at your house?"

"Because I thought you did it."

There it was, so plainly said. "After everything we've been

through together, you thought I would try to kill you?" His bloodshot eyes searched Colin's. "I tried to help you. I gave you the files you asked for."

"You knew Gwen was there. You know the paperwork was there. If we had been killed, the investigation into David's death might never be reopened."

Walker reached for his drink and realized it was empty.

Colin waved to the bartender. "Scotch on the rocks."

Gratitude welled up inside Walker as he watched the bartender pour the amber liquid. He couldn't have this conversation sober, couldn't give voice to the terrible things that needed to be said.

It occurred to him that this would be his last conversation with Colin, and he felt a profound sadness. Colin was his family. Walker had schooled him in righteousness and the law, only to be brought down by those very things he himself had admired. Again he checked his watch.

"Waiting for someone?"

"No."

"Tell me about Adele."

Walker's lips formed a hard line and he shook his head, the words locked inside like an unwilling confessor.

"I already know, but I need to hear it from you."

"Why, are you wearing a wire?"

"Nope." He leaned in close to Walker and whispered, "I looked up to you for damn near half my life, and you're a murderer and a fraud. I want to hear you say the words."

Walker could feel his lips pulling down hard at the corners, afraid he might disgrace himself and break down crying. He shot Colin a pleading look.

"Say it."

He opened his mouth to speak and felt his bottom lip shake wildly. "I killed her," he said quietly, tears welling in his eyes.

"Tell me why."

"I l-l-loved her," he choked out, the words costing him greatly. "She was pregnant, wouldn't get rid of the baby. She was going to tell June..." Walker reached for his drink and knocked it over, several people turning to stare. He brought his hand over his mouth to cover his crying.

"Why kill David? You'd gotten away with it. Everything was over."

"I panicked."

"Why?"

A fresh scotch appeared and he latched onto it. "Ahearn just got out of jail. His son hated him, but Jerry wanted to reconcile. David showed up in my office with a letter from his father, claiming his mother never contacted his grandmother."

"Did Ahearn say anything to David about you?"

Walker shook his head. "Not that I know of. But David didn't believe his dad. He thought Jerry had made Adele unhappy. He blamed his father for his mother's death. David came to see me because he wanted to know the truth. Of course, I told him she contacted her mother."

"So what's the problem?"

"He wanted proof. A piece of paper he could show his father that said he was a liar. But that paper didn't exist. That's when I realized my mistake."

Walker reflected on what he knew too well. In every crime, the perpetrator left behind clues. Some were subtle, some dramatic, and any one of them could bring him down. He sipped at his liquor without tasting it, awash in memories of the mistake that would be his undoing. "I told Jerry that Adele contacted her mother, but I never wrote it in the official file."

"You would have had to document it."

He nodded. "It was easier to write it up as a burglary. But now David was there, insisting, and I told him I couldn't give it to him. He was angry. Said he'd file a freedom of information request, go through the local police, whatever agency he had to petition, even go to the media if he had to." Walker remembered every word, every nuance in that conversation. "He said he'd throw so much light on my office it would be like sunshine in the middle of the night." He turned to Colin, his eyes beseeching. "Who knows what they would find if that happened?"

"So you killed him."

He shook his head. "I was too scared. I screwed up with Adele. This time I brought someone in."

"Who?"

"He should have been a no one. An afterthought. He should have taken his money and disappeared." Walker's voice dripped with hatred. "But he turned into the devil himself."

Colin pulled the other man around to face him. "What's his name?"

"Michael Hinman."

"Emma's boyfriend." Colin's eyes were wide. "You hired Emma's boyfriend to kill David."

Chapter 19

"He wasn't her boyfriend then. They didn't even know each other until Michael showed up on my front doorstep looking for money, and June invited him to stay for dinner."

Colin raised his hand between them. "But David recognized someone named Michael on the mountain the day he was killed. David and Michael Hinman didn't know each other."

"Sure they did. They went to the same school right down the street from my house during the Ahearn's first placement."

"Of course. You placed the family in your town to be close to Adele. That's why Jerry's request to be moved to the Southwest wasn't honored."

Walker remembered filling in the form, spelling out Connecticut in careful capital letters. Adele had meant everything to him then. He would have moved the world to be close to her. If he could have foreseen how the affair would color and destroy so many lives, he may have allowed them to relocate to Arizona as Jerry had wanted.

"I'm not proud of what I've done, Mitchell. If I could, I would change it all, if only for Emma." He shook his head. "All through dinner that punk was hitting on her, taunting me. I forbade her to see him." He remembered the first pull of the string that turned him into a marionette, a toy. "Michael called me on the phone, says I'd better change my mind if I wanted him to keep my secret." He picked up his drink. "I should have killed him then."

"Then Emma got pregnant and Michael left. Jerry Ahearn took her in."

He nodded, looking shell-shocked and old. "I know. I found her. She hated me."

"Michael stayed away until last week. He shows up at my door again, saying how come I never told him Emma had his kid. Like I should have sent him a box of cigars or something." Walker checked his watch again, nausea washing through his stomach.

"Why do you keep looking at your watch?" asked Colin.

Walker looked into his eyes like the dead, saying nothing.

Colin stood quickly. "Michael wants Luke." He looked quickly around the bar, his eyes landing on the man beside him. "Damn it, Walker! What do you know?"

"I had to do it." Walker shrugged his shoulders. "I didn't have any choice."

Colin's phone rang. "Mitchell."

"Colin, it's Emma," she was sobbing, hysterical. "Luke's gone!"

~~~

The Grand Marquis flew down the expressway like a sports car, Colin at the wheel with his one good arm and Gwen at his side. Walker was in the backseat, his hands bound in his lap with cuffs from the collection of memorabilia on the wall at Ray Flynn's. They worked well enough and had served in a pinch, but no one had a key. Rowan and Becky followed in Becky's car.

"Thank you for bringing me with you," said Walker. The alcohol and stress of his grandson's kidnapping had combined to make him weepy. "You could have left me there."

Colin felt a stab of pity for this man, even after all he had done. Walker's decision to destroy Adele had devastated his own life, a life that at one time had been good. Grief clawed at Colin as he mourned the good man he had believed Walker to be.

Somewhere out there, Luke was held hostage to a murderer. The fact that Michael was Luke's father gave Colin no comfort. Only a madman would hold his own flesh and blood for ransom. "There has to be a way to find him." Colin's eyes fixed on Walker in the mirror. "Do you have a cell phone number for Michael?"

"It showed up as unavailable," said Walker. "I looked for a cell phone listing in his name yesterday and didn't find anything."

"What did you do that for?" asked Colin.

"So I could find him and stop him once and for all."

"Why now, Graham?" asked Gwen.

He looked out the window. "I followed Colin to the house. I saw the boy, Luke. He looks like my Tommy. I wanted to protect him."

Gwen turned to Colin. "Wait, you said Michael left a prepaid cell with the ransom note?"

"Yes."

"Maybe he bought two—one for Emma and one for him to call her. Is there any way to track where he bought them and get the other number?"

"It's worth a shot," said Colin. He tossed his own cell phone to Gwen. "Call Emma back and get the number for the prepaid phone. It's on the phone's menu somewhere."

When she was finished, he said, "Now give the phone to Walker." He met Walker's eyes in the mirror. "Call the best contact you've got at the FBI and have him run it, right now."

"We'll find him," Gwen said quietly, reaching to touch Colin's arm.

Colin's emotions were running high, every nerve in his body tingling. "I let this bastard get away from me once before, and I'm sure as hell not going to let him get away again."

"It's not your fault," she said.

How could she not see it? Michael was the one who got away, slipping right through Colin's careless fingers. "This is totally my fault, Gwen. If I'd stopped this guy after he killed David, he never would have had the chance to take Luke."

They were nearly at the hospital when Colin's phone rang.

After listening for a minute, Colin swerved to the right-hand lane and talked to Gwen, the phone still held to his ear. "The phones were bought yesterday at a Wal-Mart in Quincy. They've sold twelve of that model in the last two weeks, but only one at the same time as Emma's phone. It's showing up in Chinatown."

"Where in Chinatown?" he asked into the phone.

"Thanks." He hung up the phone. "It's between Kneeland and Tyler. They're setting up a stingray to track it."

~~~

The kid was a dead ringer for Michael's brother Rick at that age, even though Michael had a hard time seeing himself in Luke's features. Rick was a jerk who used to beat on his little brother with alarming regularity, the resemblance doing little to endear Michael to his long-lost son.

Luke hadn't touched the burger and fries Michael bought for him. It cost $5.25, and he was pissed that he spent that much money for something the kid wouldn't even eat.

"Eat your burger," he said. The kid didn't move.

Michael rocked on the back two legs of a metal chair, bracing himself with the windowsill. The boy had a matching chair inside the small cell, though he was curled up in a ball in the corner of the room. He had to be ten years old, but he was acting like a baby.

Back when Michael used to work here, they stored a Bengal Tiger in the cage where Luke was locked up. They had some cool exotic animals in this place. It smelled like the animals never left, which is why the space was still vacant three years after the owner of the operation was deported. Michael lived here so long he didn't even notice the stench anymore, and certainly didn't find it as upsetting as the boy huddled in the corner.

"I said eat it!" he snapped, and was rewarded when the boy scurried to the center of the cell for the food. Luke took a large bite and chewed it slowly, his wide eyes trained on Michael's shoes.

So this is my kid.

Michael had never thought of himself as a father. He didn't use anything for birth control but he was still surprised when Emma got herself knocked up. She left town and Walker said it was taken care of, so Michael never gave it another thought until he saw Emma and the boy in the hospital cafeteria yesterday.

His parole officer set him up with the cafeteria job after he got released for grand theft auto, and since the animal shop was out of business he was stuck taking that shit job until he found something better. Then presto, in walks Emma, and he got an idea with lots of dollar signs in it.

She was there visiting some old guy, and all Michael had to do was look at the white board at the nurse's station to see who he was. Beaumont, Jerry. Same last name as the guy he'd been paid to kill by Walker. What were the odds of that?

He'd scribbled down the room number, smiling smugly. There was a reason those nurses weren't supposed to put names up there for just anybody to read.

Michael imagined money coming at him from all directions. From Emma, for sure, and from Walker to keep his mouth shut all over again. Michael wasn't sure how Jerry Beaumont played into all this, but he could only help with that financial plan.

So he'd snagged the boy.

It wasn't even hard. The trick was getting him to come voluntarily. Michael had donned a white doctor's coat and a swiped a stethoscope off a counter, then told the kid his mommy wanted him to give blood to help all the sick people in the hospital. He used Emma's name and smiled all sincere, and Luke had followed him to the basement like a puppy on the scent of a dog bone.

Luke had fought and screamed a little at the end when Michael picked him up and threw him into the van, but there wasn't anybody down there to notice.

The boy finished his burger and slunk back to the corner. "I have to go to the bathroom," he said quietly.

"Have at it, kid. I'll give you some privacy, okay?" He stood, pushing the metal chair into a metal table with a loud clang. "I ain't a pervert or nothing." He smiled, suddenly wanting the boy to know the truth. "I'm your real dad."

For the first time since Michael had kidnapped Luke, the boy put his head between his knees and cried.

~~~

Gwen looked up at a billboard for an accident lawyer as they drove, the phone number made almost entirely of threes. She didn't think much of it until she noticed the license plate on the car in front of them—333 TUH—then the sign for Route 93 and Route 3. Mentally she acknowledged the message.

Colin parked the car and put the windows down partway. "Bring the cell phone number with us in case we need it," he said to Gwen, "and grab Walker's gun from the floor."

Walker whined plaintively. "You're not leaving me here. I can help."

"I don't doubt that you could. I just don't know whose side you'd be on," said Colin, slamming the door.

He and Gwen headed for the street, the scents of cooking food and hot pavement mingling in a sickening way. "How big of an area are we looking at?" she asked.

"Right now, about two blocks. Let me call and see if they set up the Stingray."

"What's that?"

"A device that acts like a cell phone tower, but isn't. It lets us track where he is much more accurately."

"How accurately?"

"In a city with this many towers, it can tell us the building." Colin pulled out his cell phone and dialed the FBI agent he spoke with earlier. "Is the Stingray in place?" He turned to look around him, finding a street sign and turning back around. Got it." He hung up and gestured to a six or seven-story building. "That one."

They began walking and his phone rang again. It was Emma. "Michael called," she said. "He wants me to put the cash in a garbage can at the corner of Dartmouth and Beacon Streets in thirty minutes."

"Are the agents going with you?"

"He said to come alone, but they're setting up nearby."

"Be safe."

Emma sound shaky. "Have you found Luke?"

"We're still looking. I'll let you know when I have something." He hung up. "We have to hurry. The cash drop's in thirty minutes, ten minutes from here. He's going to move soon."

The building was open, but appeared to be deserted.

"Start on the third floor," Gwen said.

"Why?"

"Call it a hunch."

They located the stairwell and climbed quickly, reaching the third floor landing and quietly opening the door. The horrible smell of animal waste hit their noses.

A man's voice yelled in the distance. "I said eat it!"

Colin turned to Gwen and whispered. "I think we found Michael."

Chapter 20

Luke Beaumont was almost eleven years old, but people usually said he acted much older. He was good at taking care of things, helping his mom with the garden and the projects she liked to do around the house. He especially liked the power tools his dad kept in the garage, the drills and different saws that could take something broken and fix it up, make it look nice. His mom said next summer he could help paint the house, even climb on scaffolding and go up the ladder.

He bit at his fingernail, staring at Michael walk from one side of the expansive room to the other. Luke had heard Michael talk to his mother, calling her names that made Luke want to hurt him. Michael wanted lots of money to bring Luke home, which felt really hopeless to him as he sat in a cage in the stink of his own urine. His mom and dad didn't have a lot of money, and Luke didn't see any way he was going to get to go home.

Michael said he was Luke's father, which felt almost as bad as when his dog got hit by the car and died last year. Jerry was his father. Jerry had always been his father, even if he was Irish and Luke looked like a Sicilian. No way was this guy telling the truth.

He tasted blood and pulled his hand from his mouth, raising his head just at the right moment to see a man peeking around the corner by the elevator. Luke's head snapped back to Michael, who continued to pace, unaware they had company.

Michael's watch began an electronic alarm, an annoying tune that would forever bring Luke back to this moment in time.

"It's show time, kid." Michael peered at his cell phone as if to check. "Your mom should be dropping the money as we speak. I need to go pick it up."

Luke's stomach flipped upside-down when Michael pulled out a gun and loaded it with bullets. "What's that for?"

"Just in case your mother gets smart."

Luke's mouth went dry. "Don't hurt her."

"If she follows the rules, I won't have to."

Luke was so scared for his mom in that moment. Wouldn't there be police there? Someone to help? The police might kill Michael, and then no one would be able to find him in here. He wondered who the man by elevator was. Surely it was someone to save him?

"You'll be fine," said Michael.

"What if you don't come back?"

He ran his hand through his hair. "Jesus, kid, you ask a lot of questions. I got to go." He walked toward the elevator and Luke held his breath.

"Freeze!" the man yelled.

A gunshot erupted, the noise overwhelming in the cavernous space, and the boy's whole body jumped. Several more shots followed, then the sound of someone running and Michael reappeared, gun pointed directly at Luke.

Michael was shaking, sweat visible on his forehead. He yelled out, "You come any closer and I kill the boy!"

~~~

Colin was crouched in the shadows between a stack of packing crates and a large pile of empty cardboard boxes. He held the gun in his bad hand, not trusting himself to fire a weapon with the opposite arm. Gwen stood across the walkway, shielded from view by a tall metal cabinet. She held Walker's gun at the ready, but Colin had the better line of sight to the elevator where Michael stood.

He could hear the boy asking questions, then footsteps before Michael rounded the corner. "Freeze!" Colin yelled, watching as Michael pulled a gun from his waistband. Colin aimed for Michael's femur and pulled the trigger decisively.

Pain ripped through Colin's shoulder as the gun recoiled, and he called out involuntarily. Michael didn't seem to be hit. He returned fire, debris flying into Colin's face and eyes as the bullet struck the concrete floor, sending rocks scattering.

Colin raised a shaking hand to train his weapon on Michael and failed, the wounds to his eye and shoulder preventing him from lining up the shot. He felt panicked for Gwen. Could she handle this by herself? Defend them all and take Michael down? Reproach overwhelmed him, but he couldn't help her now.

Michael took a step toward Colin at the same instant Gwen fired, the bullet at once both hitting his shoulder and alerting him to her presence.

Colin could only make out Michael's silhouette against the wall of windows behind him, their brightness quickly dimming as his vision deteriorated. He could see Michael had been wounded from the hunch in his gait, and was proud that Gwen got a shot in. She fired again, but Michael had already turned, quickly running around the corner.

Colin knew what would come next. Luke was encaged over there. Michael Hinman got a hostage at the same moment that Colin's eyesight went completely dark.

~~~

Gwen crossed to Colin, the blood on his face making her fear for the worst. "Are you okay?"

"Go get him! He's going to get Luke!"

She stood, knowing she was already too late to stop such a thing, grateful that Colin seemed all right. Her mind raced as she stepped toward the corner.

Please help me save the boy.

Gwen often found in the most stressful situations that time was her greatest ally. She believed that time was flexible, more a construction of her own mind than any predetermined absolute. Her steps were quick and light, though in her perception the walk was interminable, stretching out as she considered what to do.

She had tools at her disposal—the weapon, her martial arts training. She had the heels of her sandals and the belt of her dress. Righteousness was on her side as well, and she wielded it like a sharply pointed sword.

Gwen took note of those who were present in spirit. David and Jerry, her own guardian angel. God himself. The boy's mother was here, as well as Rowan and Becky.

Tell me what to do.

She peered at the gun in her hand, suddenly certain she'd fare better without it, and rested it on the ground before taking the turn. She faced Michael with her empty hands raised, her blue eyes shining in the rays of the setting sun.

"You come any closer and I kill the boy!" he yelled.

Gwen could feel his stress, see the tremors that ran up his arms. Her eyes went to Luke, a huddled mass of innocent fear, his head scrunched down to his knees.

"I'm not armed," she said.

Michael's face twitched. "Where's the gun?"

"I left it back there, on the floor."

"Why?"

"God told me to."

He blew out air. "Bullshit. You probably gave it to your friend, and he's going to come around here shooting."

"Hi might." She knew Colin would if he could, but she doubted he was able. "But I won't."

Michael's brow furrowed. "What do you want?"

"To trade places with the boy."

"No."

"Let me in there with him. He's scared."

Michael looked at Luke.

Gwen could see the resemblance between father and son, hoping some scrap of the paternal bond remained. "He looks like you," she said quietly.

"He's my kid."

She took a step closer, and Michael turned the gun on her, forcing her hands higher.

"You don't move unless I tell you to move."

"Please, Michael. Let me go in with Luke. I won't be able to hurt you in there."

Luke began to sob. He took in air like he'd been crying for some time, finally unable to do it quietly.

"Stop it," said Michael.

Luke instantly cried louder, the sound echoing through the empty space.

"Stop!"

Luke's wail became hysterical.

"Let me go to him," Gwen said loudly. "I can calm him down."

"Okay, okay." Michael took a key out of his pocket. "Stop fucking crying!" He unlocked the gate and Gwen stepped forward.

In Gwen's mind, she sauntered instead of walked, planning her attack. Michael held the gate wide for her to enter, the distance between her foot and his face so perfectly measured as to be considered a gift. Gwen shifted her weight to one side and lifted her other leg, kicking Michael soundly in the throat with the pointed heel of her sandal.

He hit the concrete face first, the sound a sickening smack.

She made sure he was dead, then turned to the boy in the cell. "It's okay now, sweetheart. He can't hurt you anymore." She opened her arms and Luke ran to her, taller and older than she'd been expecting. "Come. We need to call for help."

The pair jogged back to the elevator where Colin sat on the floor, blood streaming from his face. "Gwen?"

"And Luke."

"Michael?"

"He's dead."

"Thank God you're okay." He took his cell phone out of his pocket and handed it to her. "You'll have to make the call. I can't see a damned thing."

~~~

There was a knock on the open door.

"Can we come in?"

Colin couldn't place the voice, the bandages over his eyes making him completely blind. With any luck, it was a temporary inconvenience and not a permanent disability.

"Of course," said Gwen. She touched his hand and said quietly, "It's Emma and Luke."

"How are you feeling, Colin?" asked Emma.

"Pretty good," he lied smoothly. "They think the vision will come back as everything heals up." There was some truth to that. The doctors were confident at least one of his eyes would see again.

Luke was beside Colin, closer than he realized. "Thank you for saving me."

"You're welcome, buddy, but it was Gwen who really saved you."

"Thank you too, Miss Gwen."

"You're most welcome, Luke."

"How's Jerry doing?" Colin asked.

"He's great," said Emma. "Up and walking around already."

Luke shuffled his feet. "He told me I need a haircut."

"They might discharge him in the morning," said Emma. "He's going to need physical therapy for a while, but the doctor expects him to make a full recovery."

"Oh, what a relief," said Gwen. "I'll bet you want him home."

"Yes, I really do," said Emma.

Becky's overly loud voice joined the chorus. "Howdy kids."

Emma and Luke said their goodbyes, heading upstairs to visit with Jerry until his release, and Becky plopped down on the hospital bed at Colin's feet. "I got you something."

Something light landed on his lap and he picked it up, a stuffed animal of some sort.

"It's a bat."

He smiled at her sense of humor. "Blind as a bat. You shouldn't have."

"I really wanted a mole, because technically speaking, they're the only truly blind animal, according to Wikipedia. But no one sells stuffed moles. Apparently they're not cute or cuddly enough. And," she said with a flourish, "I brought you cake."

"What kind?" he asked.

"Carrot, cheese, chocolate and homemade rum spice made with real rum, thank you very much. I wasn't sure what you liked."

He chose some of each cake and made small talk with the people who cared about him. It was several hours later when Colin had to admit defeat. "I was trying to wait for Rowan, but I'm tired." His brother was headed back to Italy on a late flight this evening.

"It's been a long few days," Gwen said. "Get some rest. I'll wake you when he gets here."

Colin slept heavily, with strange dreams of a warehouse full of bats turning into seagulls on the beach. Quiet talking woke him slowly.

"I still miss him." It was Rowan, the sadness in his voice nearly palpable.

"As do I," said Gwen. "I've felt him around me more in the past few days than I have in the past few years. It reminded me of how much I still love that man." She sighed heavily. "I'll be in love with David Beaumont until I'm an old woman, crossing over the River Styx and running into his waiting arms."

The emotion in Gwen's voice was so powerful, her love so profound. Colin's heart ached. Could there be room in Gwen's heart for any other man?

"Is that ridiculous?" she asked. "I've had that image in my head for so long. I can almost imagine it happening."

"You two were something special. That kind of love doesn't come around every day."

"And what about you?" she asked. "Your wife?"

"It's complicated, Gwen."

"Do you love her?"

He whistled between his teeth. "Don't know."

"Now that, I can relate to. It's not always easy to tell what love has in store for us, is it?"

"Definitely not."

Colin knew she was talking about him, and her ambivalence was like a slap to the face. He had known he wanted Gwen Trueblood since the moment he first met her, yet she was still uncertain. It seemed her indecision was a decision in itself.

"I wish you well, my friend," said Gwen. "Are you sure you don't want me to wake him so you can say goodbye?"

"Nah. I'll call him in a day or two once we're both home."

"I'll give him your love. Have a safe journey."

"I will. Bye, Gwen."

Chapter 21

Colin paced from the window of his hospital room to the hallway and back again. His left eye was bandaged but his right was revealed, allowing him to see despite the healing wounds around it. He had showered this morning and dressed in anticipation of being discharged, but the hour was getting later and no one had come with the paperwork.

"Good morning," said Gwen, carrying a tray of coffee and something wrapped in waxed paper. "You're up! How are your eyes?"

Good enough to take in the pretty picture she made, her hair whipped up off her shoulders, wearing a gauzy white tank top that ended at her hip in layers of generous ruffles. He stared at her, trying to memorize her face, the blue of her eyes, the curve of her jaw.

"The right one seems fine. The left, not so much."

"Did the doctor say anything?"

"Just that we have to wait and see. They're sending me home."

Gwen picked up a coffee and handed it to him. "I got bagels with lox from a delicatessen down the street. They're sinful, they're so good. Here, taste." She put the bagel to his lips, but he turned away.

"Gwen…"

"Yes?"

"I'm going home."

"That's good news."

He shook his head, rubbing his hand through his hair. "No, I mean, I'm going back to Cold Spring."

She dropped her hand. "What are you saying?"

She looked so vulnerable. He loved her completely, the knowledge only serving to make this more painful. He reached out and gently wiped her cheek with his fingertips. "I'm saying that I don't think we should see each other anymore."

Gwen stared back at him, her bottom lip falling into a

cupid's bow. "I don't understand, Colin. What changed between us? I thought you loved me."

I thought you loved me.

She probably didn't even realize she'd said it. "I do love you, Gwen, and it's killing me to say this, but you don't have enough room in *your* heart to love two men at the same time."

She turned around, putting her hands on her hips. "David."

"Yes."

"He's been dead for twelve years, Colin. Twelve years! Are you really implying I haven't moved on with my life, that I can't love again?"

"That's exactly what I'm saying."

A nurse walked in, placing a stack of papers on the tray table. "Colin Mitchell?"

"Yes."

"I have your discharge paperwork. Have a seat, please, so we can go through it."

Two and a half hours he'd been waiting, and she comes at the worst possible moment. "Can you come back in a little while?"

Gwen raised her hand. "Not on my account. I was just leaving anyway."

"Gwen…"

She raised steely eyes to his. "It's fine, Colin." She pulled sunglasses out of her purse and put them on. "I trust you will have a safe trip home and a speedy recovery."

He wanted to stop her, to beg her to stay, but all he could say was, "Thank you."

"Goodbye, Colin."

Colin watched as the woman he loved for half his life turned on her heel and walked out of it.

~~~

Gwen knelt in the freshly cut grass, digging a hole with a small trowel. Her gardening gloves were heavily soiled, her work here near complete. Reaching for the plastic pot, she loosened the roots of a bright yellow chrysanthemum and set the bushy plant into the ground.

"I know you love marigolds, but they're not in season," she

said to the plaque, now clearly visible in the tidy cemetery. It had taken her nearly a week to reclaim the overgrown space, the addition of flowers and some shrubbery making the area more beautiful and serene. "I think Lucy likes the color."

Gwen stood and brushed off her long legs, dirty circles still clinging to the skin of her knees. She put her hand over her eyes to shield them from the sun, and took in the expanse of her property.

She would miss it here.

Her work to ready the house for sale was complete. The porch swing had received a coat of red paint, sharply setting off the white house with its new green shutters. Gone were her more flamboyant art installations, leaving only a small sculpture of a young woman in the garden to watch over the rolling hillside in her stead.

The house didn't look like her own anymore. Funny how homes sell faster when they look like no one with any personality lives in them.

She walked to the shed and replaced the gardening tools, as a small red convertible pulled into the drive. A tiny woman with long black hair and very high black heels stepped out of the car. "It's open house day!" she shouted, coming close to Gwen for an airy hug. "Are you ready?"

"Oh, I'm ready all right. How are you, Beverly?"

"I'm good, thanks for asking. The porch swing looks fabulous. I love the red." She held out her hand, wiggling her fingers. "Did you pack up the…other things?"

The 'other things' consisted of everything Gwen owned that could not be bought at a superstore. Beverly called it "de-cluttering". It had taken a monumental effort, an enormous storage unit and the help of two high school kids Gwen hired from town.

"I did. I think you'll find everything very neutral."

Many of the things in the house had belonged to David, making Gwen realize how much letting go she still had to accomplish. It had taken her only a week to organize everything and donate it to various charities, but the emotional journey had taken her the balance of the summer and fall.

No wonder Colin had sent her away, insisting she was still in love with her husband's ghost. In some ways, she had never let him go. Gwen had fooled herself into believing she was living her life fully, simply because she was no longer huddled in a corner, actively grieving her husband's death. But she had not opened herself up again to love and the wonders it could bring, somehow living in the small space between the two extremes.

"I'm just going to take a quick shower and be on my way," Gwen said, turning to walk into the house.

"Wonderful." Beverly flashed an overly white smile. "It's a beautiful home. It's going to go quickly, Gwen."

"Yes, I think it will." Gwen smiled and headed upstairs, her hands lovingly caressing the wooden banister. She had become a bride here, been a wife to her husband here, planned a family that had never been realized within these walls.

She was ready to leave it behind, like a winter coat in the spring. Excitement bubbled within her, anxious and alive. Gwen didn't know what the future held in store, but she couldn't wait to find out.

~~~

Colin had sailed all the way to Poughkeepsie, making the most of a perfect fall day. The sun shone brightly, not a cloud in the sky, with a dream wind that effortlessly pushed his eighteen-foot boat further than he had intended to travel. He made his way back slowly, in no hurry to dock and face another night alone at the quiet marina.

Construction of the house was going well, the foundation cured and the framing for the first floor nearly completed. The architect had worked from old pictures to recreate the lighthouse-like turret, though Colin had designed the rest of the house to suit himself, with larger open spaces and modern conveniences.

The project had consumed the bulk of his energy since returning from Boston, providing him with something to do outside of work and thinking about Gwen. Colin knew he did the right thing sending her away, but when he couldn't sleep for thinking of her, he cursed himself with every toss and turn. Was it really so important that she love him more than a dead man?

It was.

And so the days were long and nights were longer, the house he would occupy alone designed for the woman who would never set foot inside its walls, with an art studio no one would paint in and a nursery for a baby who would never exist.

~~~

Music flowed on the air, the sound of a string quartet. Gwen thought it was Mozart, but she couldn't be sure. Her feet followed the stone pavers as she listened, her sandals quietly clicking in time to the tune.

She thought of the last time was here, just a few months ago, so dreading her confrontation with Colin. Gwen knew now that she had been afraid, scared that he would awaken feelings that would require her to change.

The doors to the Chapel Restoration stood open in welcome, much as they had on her first visit to this magical place. Climbing the steps, Gwen let the sounds surround her, true happiness welling inside her soul. This was where she belonged, where she wanted to live for all time, with Colin by her side.

Would he have her?

She was grateful he had sent her away, refusing to accept only half of her heart. She had kept the memory of her husband held tightly in her clutches, which was not how David would have wanted her to live. To love again was to honor his memory, to carry on joyfully a testament to life itself.

But she wasn't doing this for David. Gwen's love for Colin was strong and true, completely separate from all that had come before. She hoped they would make a life, become a family in this little town on the banks of the Hudson River.

Gwen opened her eyes and stepped into the Chapel, the pews decorated with fall-colored chrysanthemums and yellow bows in preparation for a wedding. She smiled as she thought of Crystal, and hoped the flowers were for the young woman's much-anticipated celebration.

The music began to crescendo, making the hair on Gwen's arms stand up on end with its beauty. She stood in awe of the sounds, their majesty and tenor, frozen as she listened to the final chord and the silence that followed.

"Bravo!" she yelled out as she clapped. "Belissimo!"

A touch on her arm made her swiftly turn around. Colin stood before her, a look of wonder taking over his suntanned features.

Gwen smiled widely, so surprised she nearly laughed out loud. How good it was to see his handsome face, to feel his warm brown eyes connect with hers so intimately. "Colin, what are you doing here?"

"I live here."

She giggled. "No, I mean in the Chapel. I was heading to your house next, but you surprised me."

"There isn't much of a house there anymore."

"I figured I'd ask around until I found you."

The violinist began to play a quick jaunty tune, and Colin touched her elbow, steering her to the door. "Let's go outside."

Her pulse raced at his ordinary touch, so excited was she to be near him again. They stepped onto the porch, a gentle breeze bringing the scents of fall leaves and flowers to her nose. "Where are you living, then?"

"On my boat." He gestured with his chin. "The marina's right over there. The house is being rebuilt. I was on my way over to check on their progress when I heard the music. Gwen, what are you doing here?"

"I love it here. I stopped by on the way to your house last time, too."

"No, not the Chapel. Why are you here in town?"

"To see you."

He stared at her, waiting for an explanation.

She opened her mouth to speak, tears instantly burning at the back of her eyes. "I missed you."

Colin turned to stare at the river.

"I was angry with you when you sent me away," she continued. "I didn't understand why. But then I got back to Vermont and I realized that I did understand. I understood completely."

He turned back to look at her.

"I had to let go of David before I could really love you."

"Yes."

She nodded, letting a single tear slip down her cheek. "I've been working on it." She laughed. "There was a lot to do, and it's taken some time. I hope you didn't give up on me."

He stepped closer. "Never."

"Good. Because I love you, Colin. And I want to be with you forever." Then his lips were on hers and joy burst into her heart, reunited with this man who meant everything and more.

His head came up so he peered into her eyes. "I didn't even dare to dream you might come back." He rocked with her, pressing his forehead to hers. "You've made me so happy. Do you know?"

"I'm staying, too. I hope it's a big boat."

He laughed. "We could go to your house."

"My Realtor just called. It sold for full asking price about an hour ago."

His head snapped up. "What? You sold your house?"

"I did." She beamed at him, happier than she could remember being in a very long while.

"You're serious. You're really going to stay."

"Oh yes, Colin. I'm really going to stay."

~~~

They were anchored off the shore near Storm King Mountain, the setting sun casting a pink glow upon the opposite shore. Colin held a chrysanthemum in one hand and Gwen in the other, spinning the flower by its stem as he gently rubbed the bare skin of her back.

"It was nice of Crystal to let us use her flowers," murmured Gwen.

He kissed the top of her head. He had proposed on the porch of the Chapel Restoration, seeing no reason to wait when everything he wanted was there for the asking. Crystal and her husband were their witnesses.

"Can I tell you something?" he asked.

"Hmm?"

"During the ceremony, when I turned to you to say my vows, I saw someone in the doorway at the back of the church."

She raised her head, a smile spreading across her lips. "I saw him too."

"He gave me a thumbs-up."

Gwen sat up and flung her leg over his torso. "He probably thinks you have excellent taste in women."

He reached up to touch her. "I love you, Gwen. I'm going to be a good husband to you. Make you happy."

She kissed his palm. "You already make me happy."

"I want to give you a baby."

She looked around the tiny cabin, laughing. "Where on earth would we put it?"

He thought of the blue prints, the nursery with the window overlooking the valley. "Oh, I think we can find someplace."

Made in the USA
Las Vegas, NV
07 December 2024

13392049R00090